***There were a few things a living, breathing male wasn't equipped to resist...***

And at the top of the list was a beautiful woman who smelled like sin and who wanted to be touched.

I swallowed thickly and slipped my hands from Molly's lush hips to wrap them around her waist. She felt so good tucked against my body that I didn't want the moment to end. My throbbing erection rested against her trembling stomach, making me want far more, but I restrained myself. Something I wasn't used to doing.

I knew that if I wanted, I could have her. Walk her back to her hotel nearby and seduce my way into her bed. But some invisible force held me back. Her reaction a moment ago when she'd accidentally made contact with my police-issue firearm had shuddered through me as surely as if I was the one who'd had a cold bucket of reality dumped over my head.

I felt her hands move from where they were plastered against my back. Her fingertips worked their way under the hem of my shirt and touched my bare skin. I sucked in a breath.

"You'd better decide, Molly. Because in two seconds there won't be a decision to make...."

Blaze™

Dear Reader,

When it comes to sequels, we all know that it's hard to top the story that's come before. But in this third and final installment in our DANGEROUS LIAISONS miniseries...well, let's just say that our characters made our job easy, providing an explosive conclusion that pulls all three books together.

In *Submission,* darkly sexy homicide detective Alan Chevalier is at the end of his rope in both his career and his personal life. So far he's arrested the wrong man, looked in all the wrong places, and the Quarter Killer seems to have singled him out for taunting. Facts that Molly, city outsider and the all-too-tempting twin sister of the first victim, won't let him forget...in bed or out.

We hope you enjoy this journey through the minds and hearts of Alan and Molly. We'd love to hear what you think. Contact us at P.O. Box 12271, Toledo, OH 43612 (we'll respond with a signed bookplate, newsletter and bookmark), or visit us on the Web at www.toricarrington.net for fun drawings.

Here's wishing you love, romance and *hot* reading.

*Lori and Tony Karayianni*

aka Tori Carrington

# TORI CARRINGTON

## *Submission*

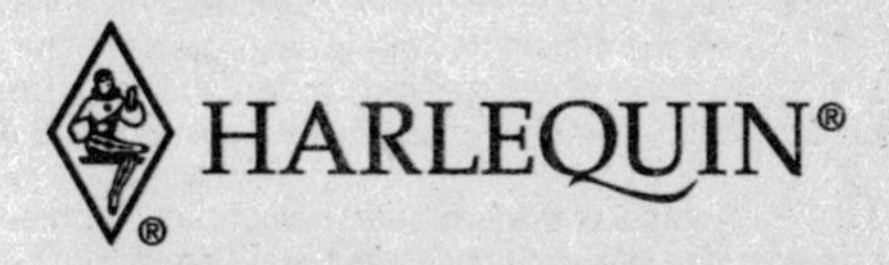


TORONTO • NEW YORK • LONDON
AMSTERDAM • PARIS • SYDNEY • HAMBURG
STOCKHOLM • ATHENS • TOKYO • MILAN • MADRID
PRAGUE • WARSAW • BUDAPEST • AUCKLAND

ISBN 0-373-79253-0

SUBMISSION



This edition published by arrangement with Harlequin Books S.A.



www.eHarlequin.com

**Printed in U.S.A.**

## ABOUT THE AUTHOR

Bestselling, multi-award-winning duo Lori and Tony Karayianni have published over thirty novels under the pen name Tori Carrington. They are two-time finalists for the prestigious Romance Writers of America's RITA® Award, and their personal motto is "Have laptop, will travel!" Look for the authors—and if you're lucky, a tray of Tony's Famous Baklava—at bookstores and conferences in your neck of the woods. For more info on Lori and Tony and their titles, visit them on the Web at www.toricarrington.net or write to them at P.O. Box 12271, Toledo, Ohio 43612.

## Books by Tori Carrington

### HARLEQUIN BLAZE

15—YOU SEXY THING!
37—A STRANGER'S TOUCH
56—EVERY MOVE YOU MAKE
65—FIRE AND ICE
73—GOING TOO FAR
105—NIGHT FEVER
109—FLAVOR OF THE MONTH
113—JUST BETWEEN US…
129—FORBIDDEN
137—INDECENT
145—WICKED
212—POSSESSION
243—OBSESSION

### HARLEQUIN TEMPTATION

837—NEVER SAY NEVER AGAIN
876—PRIVATE INVESTIGATIONS
890—SKIN DEEP
924—RED-HOT & RECKLESS

We dedicate this book wholeheartedly
to two people we encounter nearly every day—
postal workers Jeanne Murphy and Sandi Weaks.
You both make the mundane something
to look forward to. Thank you!

And to Brenda Chin's boys, Kenai and Koda,
for inspiring a special "character" in this book.

# 1

A SOUND AS GRATING AS A woman's fingernails scratching against a chalkboard wrenched me from sleep. I pulled my pillow over my head and tried to ignore it. But like my ex-wife, it refused to go away.

I snaked a hand out from under the pillow, then dragged the telephone receiver to my ear. "What?"

"Detective Alan Chevalier, please."

"That would be me."

"Sir, we have a possible three-zero." The dispatcher stated the address of the homicide.

I mumbled something that she must have taken as an okay because she hung up. On my end, it took three tries before I finally got the receiver back into the cradle. In one move I hauled the pillow from my face and sat up, then stared blearily at the closed shades drawn tight against the windows, the edges ablaze with the morning sunlight slamming against them. I squinted at the digital clock half turned away from me on the nightstand. Just after eight in the morning.

Damn.

I was late starting my normal weekday. Although the definition of *normal* was up for grabs.

Sometimes being a homicide detective in New Orleans's Eighth Precinct, French Quarter, wasn't all it was cracked up to be.

Sometimes? Lately I'd come to view my job as a necessary evil. Necessary because, since I presently lacked the pleasure of a big-busted blonde to wake me up in the middle of the night, what else would I do with my time? Evil because lately I didn't look much better than the victims of a killer who didn't want to be found.

I stared at my morning erection, feeling part of yet separate from the organ that had gotten me into more trouble than it was worth. I covered it by putting on the slacks lying on the floor and then I moved into the bathroom on autopilot. Standing in front of the bathroom mirror, I wasn't entirely certain what was to blame for the blurriness—the grimy mirror or the half bottle of bourbon I'd downed last night. I flicked on the light, winced at the ice pick it stuck into my skull, then switched it back off, relying on the bedside lamp in the other room to cast enough light for me to do what I had to. Which, admittedly, wasn't much. A quick splash of water over a face that women called full of character but never handsome (although recently they hadn't called it much of anything at all because women didn't much factor into my life as of late): green eyes that were often mistaken for brown, sandy brown hair a month overdue for a cut and lines that may have once been laugh lines but were now just wear and tear.

I scraped my palm against the stubble on my jaw. I could get away with another day of not shaving. Anyway, a dead body waited. And while it wouldn't be going anywhere anytime soon, there would be others waiting for me to do my job so they could do theirs. And while my appearance wasn't much of a priority for me, my job was. Simply because I wanted to keep it.

Shortly thereafter I walked down the two flights of stairs to the street and stood fighting against the bright morning sunlight to keep my eyes open. An interesting percentage of the Quarter's denizens—and an even bigger chunk of visitors—liked to think of themselves as vampires. With my present aversion to sunlight, I could have been bitten by one last night.

But I knew the only thing I was cursed with was a wicked hangover.

I stepped toward my twelve-year-old navy blue Chevy Caprice, a solid car, if unsightly. A bit like me, I supposed.

Only this morning it bore a hood ornament I wasn't used to seeing. Well, at least not without a price tag attached. And I was pretty sure that the attractive woman leaning against the front of my car wasn't a streetwalker, if only because her clothes revealed she was from a place where autumn required a change in wardrobe. A wool suit in New Orleans in October would immediately peg anyone as an outsider. And this girl, no matter how hot, was definitely an outsider.

She spotted me when I took my keys out of my pocket and unlocked the driver's-side door.

"Detective Chevalier?"

She knew me. Which usually meant bad news. A looker like this one, and I didn't recognize her? Could mean one of two things: I'd met her when I'd had too much to drink or she was associated with someone else I'd met when I'd had too much to drink.

I squinted up into her face and my stomach pitched. Because I wasn't only looking at an outsider; I was looking at a dead woman. Claire Laraway. My unsolved-murder victim from two weeks ago.

"Are you all right, Detective?" She blinked as if a thought had just occurred to her. "I'm sorry. Sometimes I forget how much my sister and I looked alike. I'm Molly Laraway, Claire's twin sister. We're fraternal, not identical, but we still always looked enough alike to… I didn't mean to startle you."

Startle me? Christ, she had me wondering if there was something to the upcoming Halloween celebration, one of the longest nights of the year in the city of the dead when it was believed that ghosts walked the earth.

"I was hoping I could talk to you," she said.

The only thing that could be worse than confronting the ghost of a victim whose murder you hadn't solved was dealing with the sibling of one.

I inserted the key into the car door and opened it. "Call the office."

I climbed inside, but a cleverly positioned bag with sequins on it prevented me from closing the door. "I *have* called the office. Countless times. And I always get the same response—I'll hear something when there's something to hear."

I grimaced, recognizing the words as my own.

It wasn't that I was a cold person. It was just that in my job nearly every victim came with well-meaning relatives attached. Wives, husbands, children, friends. And they all thought the killing of their loved ones elevated them to detective status; at best, making themselves pests; at worst, hindering my investigation.

I stared at her bag and where it was still stuck in my door. I hadn't meant to go farther than that, but I found my gaze taking in the fullness of her breasts beneath the brown wool of her jacket, the flare of her hips, the length of her legs—which looked great in heels not too high to be impractical but not too short to be sexy.

"Detective Chevalier, I need to know what's going on in the investigation of my sister's death. I want to help find her killer."

I moved her bag out of the way. "Go home, Miss Laraway, and let me do my job."

She replaced the bag with fingers I couldn't exactly slam in the door. "From what I can see, you're not doing that job very well."

Now that would get her far. Pretty much as far as she'd gotten.

"Remove your hands from my vehicle, Miss Laraway, before I remove them for you."

She stared at me as if gauging my willingness to do just that. She removed her fingers.

I closed the door and started the engine.

A knock at the window.

I pushed the button to open it a crack.

"Here," she said, holding a card through the slit. "This is my contact information. I'm staying at the Ritz."

I didn't take the card.

She didn't retract it.

"Detective Chevalier, I think it only fair to warn you that I'm not going anywhere. I'm here for the duration. However long it takes to find my sister's killer."

"Alan," I said automatically.

I took the card.

She smiled at me.

I wished I hadn't taken the card.

"I'd like to treat you to lunch today if you can spare the time," she said.

"I'm busy."

"Dinner, then."

I thought of the two nickels I had in my pocket and grimaced.

"Coffee?"

"Look, Miss Laraway, I don't know what you hope to accomplish by coming down here from…"

"Toledo."

Was that even a real place? I thought it was something made up on TV. "The best way you can help is by letting me do my job."

"How does coffee prevent you from doing your job?"

My hangover-dulled mind couldn't produce a response to that.

She said, "Eleven o'clock, then. At Tujague's in the French Quarter."

Tujague's happened to serve the best beef rémoulade in New Orleans, if not the whole of Louisiana. And it had been a while since I'd had it.

I knew I should refuse the invite. But damn if I could come up with a real good reason why.

"I'll be there if I have the time."

I put the car into gear and pulled away, looking into the rearview mirror at the woman with legs that went all the way up to her beautiful neck. I told myself she was nothing but trouble with a capital *T.*

But it had been a long time since I'd gotten myself into that kind of trouble. And so long as she wasn't married to my superior, well, maybe this kind of trouble was just what I needed….

MOLLY LARAWAY STOOD staring after the departing Chevy, feeling frustrated and defeated and intrigued all at once. Detective Alan Chevalier was everything and nothing she'd imagined him to be. Oh, the cavalier attitude she'd expected, since she'd received as much from him on the phone. But there was something more about the rumpled man, something that niggled under her too-warm jacket and her damp skin. Something that made her itch more than the worsted wool did.

She glanced at her watch. She'd been in town since yesterday morning and, aside from coaxing the detective's home address out of a desk sergeant at the Eighth Precinct with a few crisp bills and collecting her sister's things from FBI agent Akela Brooks, she hadn't accomplished a lot. Of course, what had she expected? To come down here and have Chevalier lay the case out on a table in front of her? To see a pattern in the evidence and immediately pinpoint the killer's identity?

"I don't know why you're wasting your time, girl," her mother had said last night when Molly had called her from the hotel to tell her where she was. "You always were a little too ambitious for your own good."

She'd heard the sentence more times than she could count over her twenty-seven years, but she'd always taken it as a compliment. At least someone in their family was determined to do something with her life.

But last night she'd taken the comment as an insult.

Probably because she'd been in a strange room in a strange city, alone and without anything to occupy her but the box of Claire's meager belongings.

She realized she was still standing on the street staring after a car that had long since left. She'd found herself in similar positions in the past two and a half weeks—being somewhere and forgetting why she was there and where she needed to go next. But right now, part of the reason was that she didn't have anywhere to go next.

Her head jerked up, a chill running up the backs of her arms. She had the odd sensation that she was being watched. She scanned the windows of the houses and apartments squashed together on the narrow street. Not a face or a moving curtain among them.

She regained her bearings and turned around, going back the way she'd come, toward the spot where the taxi had let her off near the French Quarter.

Where should she go next?

It was said that twins shared a special connection, but she'd never really believed it. Claire had. She'd spent many a conversation trying to convince Molly that she knew how she felt, what she was thinking. But while Claire may have had some sort of insight into her thoughts and feelings, Molly had never understood the same of her sister. When they were younger, Claire had spent the majority of her time outdoors—usually with boys—while Molly had stayed indoors, taking care of the house while their mother worked or reading in the room she shared with her twin. When they were in high school, Claire had dated the football captain and had gone to all the "in" parties, while Molly had studied hard, graduating at the top of their class. She'd been offered scholarships at three different universities and had picked the one closest to home for practical reasons.

No, she'd never felt any sort of paranormal connection to her twin sister…until two and a half weeks ago.

Molly caught herself rubbing her neck. She'd known the instant Claire had died. Had felt the knife that had taken her twin's life as surely as if the cold blade had been pressed against her own throat. Had experienced her sister's horror, dread, then felt the life slipping from her body just as the blood had flowed from her wound.

Every minute of every day Molly felt her twin's ghost haunting her, demanding that she find her killer.

And Molly intended to do exactly that. Either with or without Detective Chevalier's help.

# 2

I PULLED THE OLD CHEVY to the curb outside Hotel Josephine in the old section of the French Quarter. The place had become familiar to me lately. Not because I'd ever stayed there but because just over two weeks ago another body had shown up in one of the rooms. A body that had looked remarkably like the woman I'd just left standing in the street outside my apartment.

I got out of the car, grabbed my hat from the front seat, then stood staring at the four-story structure not unlike countless others in the Quarter. It was probably at least two centuries old—and looked it.

A uniformed NOPD officer who'd arrived on the scene before me hiked up his pants as I approached the door.

"What do we got?" I asked.

"Thirty-C. Room 2B."

Damn. The thirty indicated homicide. The C indicated homicide by cutting, which meant this victim might very well be connected to the one before.

The pretty hotel owner, Josie Villefranche, was

standing near the front desk, her honey-colored skin looking pale. Not that I could blame her. I'd heard business had taken a nosedive after the first unsolved murder. Now that there was a second, Lord only knew how she'd manage to keep afloat.

"Miss Villefranche," I said.

"Detective Chevalier."

I knew she kept an illegal sawed-off shotgun behind the front desk, which probably explained why she was partial to standing near it at all times.

Since I couldn't ask questions until I actually had them to ask, I climbed the stairs to the second floor. Another uniformed officer stood outside the door to 2B, guarding it.

"John," I said, recognizing him.

"Alan."

I stepped into the doorway and stared inside the room. And for the second time that day I saw a ghost. Because the victim stretched across the bed, her head hanging over the foot, was in the same position and had the same throat wound as Claire Laraway.

I'd never been one to buy into coincidence. If it looked like a crawfish, smelled like a crawfish and tasted like a crawfish...well, it was a goddamn crawfish.

I rubbed my closed eyelids and took a deep breath, then stepped farther into the room, pushing aside the similarities between the last victim and this one and instead focusing on the differences. Number one, I knew this victim. Her name was Frederique Arkart and she was a streetwalker, not a new resident to the city. Number two, she was African-American. I slowly crouched down, taking in the way her eyes seemed to stare at a point I couldn't see. For all intents and purposes, she couldn't see it, either, but it was apparent that she'd been looking at something—or rather someone—while her life was being taken away from her. I blindly reached for a rubber glove in the pocket of my trench coat and put it on my right hand. Number three, the wounds were different, I found as I lightly probed the victim's neck. Laraway's had been made with a sharp instrument, while the blade used here had been duller, making a sloppy job of it.

I took off the glove and sat crouched for long minutes, staring at the floor in front of me.

New Orleans ranked pretty high in the nation when it came to murder statistics. I knew this not because I read the papers but because I was kept busier than most other detectives in bigger cities. I'd seen more than my share of murders and had no fewer than a dozen actively open cases sitting on my desk at any one time, with a countless number of others that had been marked cold cases and filed away.

"Looks familiar."

I craned my neck to look at the chief of forensics, Steven Chan, then stood up. "Yeah."

"You think we're dealing with the same killer?"

He put his box down in a corner where it was least likely there would be any trace evidence.

"That's your job, not mine."

"Well, that's the first time I've heard you say that."

He was right. Usually I would be telling him that it looked as though the wounds were different somehow. But I thought it was a good idea if I was a little more careful nowadays. I'd arrested the wrong man in the Laraway murder and didn't want to be placed in that position again anytime soon. Especially considering that my career already hung by a very thin thread.

"Let me know what you come up with," I said. "I'm going down to talk to the owner."

MOLLY SAT AT A BACK table at Tujague's and stared at her watch. It was a quarter after eleven and Detective Chevalier was late.

Either that or he'd never planned to come.

"Decide yet?" the young waiter asked.

"I'm waiting for someone," she said again.

He smiled at her in a way that said he knew she was waiting but he'd approached her to see if she'd given up and decided to eat anyway.

She pulled a menu in front of her.

A cordially shouted greeting drew her attention toward the door. She was mildly surprised to find Alan Chevalier stepping inside, his overcoat as wrinkled as it had been earlier, holding his hat as he shook hands with the portly man behind the bar—apparently the issuer of the hearty welcome.

Molly was both glad and nervous that he'd decided to come. The mix of reactions intrigued her. His being there meant he might include her in the investigation, or at the very least keep her informed on his progress.

Her gaze mingled with his across the already crowded dining room and she swallowed hard, aware now, as she had been earlier, of the strange chemistry that seemed to exist between them.

His being there also meant that he might feel the same pull.

It took him a few moments to make it to the table. She expected him to take off his overcoat—her own wool jacket was on the back of her chair—but he didn't. He merely sat back in his chair, staring at her silently, his arm stretched out so that the hand that held his hat lay on the table between them.

"I'm glad you could make it," she said quietly.

He didn't say anything, almost as if he was as surprised to be there as she was to see him there.

Finally he leaned forward and placed his hat on the empty chair to his right. "Yes, well, this happens to be one of my favorite places. I might have been planning on coming here anyway."

Molly had given up all pretense of reading the menu and looked him over instead. She'd noticed this morning that he'd looked a little ragged around the edges. It had been at least a day since he'd shaved, and he was in need of a haircut. His clothes…well, it looked as if he might have slept in them, the wrinkles and creases speaking of a man who was either too busy to make or uninterested in making an effort with his appearance.

Strangely this lack of concern for the way he looked appealed to her on a level she hadn't been aware of until now. She usually went for the well-groomed types. Career-driven, gym-obsessed overachievers in pressed suits who carried expensive briefcases and drove cars that cost more than some houses.

But Alan Chevalier…

She realized she was staring and dropped her gaze to the white tablecloth.

"Has anything—" she began, then stopped, realizing the futile nature of her question.

"Happened in your sister's case since I saw you a couple of hours ago?" He shook his head. "No."

"Hello, Detective Chevalier. The usual?" the young waiter asked the man across from her.

"Yes," he said. "And bring the same for the lady." He considered her. "Unless you're a vegetarian?"

Molly said that whatever he'd ordered was fine.

The waiter disappeared, leaving them alone again.

Well, *alone* really wasn't the applicable word. The small restaurant was packed with other diners, despite the early hour. But as far as Molly was concerned, they could have been alone in the popular eatery.

"So, Miss Laraway, what is it that you do for a living?"

"I'm a lawyer."

His eyebrows rose.

"You seem surprised."

"Your career doesn't impact me one way or another, Miss Laraway." He shrugged. "Which branch of law?"

"Right now I'm assigned to business law at the firm where I work."

"But you hope to…"

"Eventually move on to criminal law."

He nodded, as if expecting the answer. "A defense attorney."

"Is there something wrong with that?"

He looked over her suit as if trying to put the pieces of her together. "Getting off the same people I bust my ass trying to put behind bars?" He shook his head. "No, I don't have a problem with that."

Molly tucked a strand of blond hair behind her ear. "Anyway, my career isn't the reason we're here, is it?"

"Ah, yes." He leaned forward, folding his hands on top of the table. "Your sister."

Had he forgotten?

She realized with some interest that it appeared he had. And that he didn't seem concerned about the fact, either.

An unwelcome thrill raced through her bloodstream as her gaze took in his hands. Strong hands, clean, nails clipped and neat, dark hair peppering the backs of his thick, square fingers. They were capable hands, manly.

And she was paying them far too much attention.

Molly cleared her throat and took a notepad from her bag.

"Were you and your sister close, Miss Laraway?"

"Molly, please." She pulled out a pen and laid it against the pad. "And, no, unfortunately my sister and I were never very close. Despite the belief about twins, she and I were nothing alike. And when she moved down here last year, we pretty much fell out of touch."

She didn't like admitting that. Seeing as they'd been the only two siblings in their single-parent household, she thought she should have made more of an effort. Called her sister. E-mailed her. At least kept track of how she was doing.

"Do you know if she was dating anyone at the time of her death?"

Molly shook her head, unable to bring herself to meet his gaze.

"Isn't that the type of thing a sister—forget a twin—would usually know?"

"Do you have any siblings, Detective Chevalier?"

He seemed taken aback by her response. "That's not at issue here."

"And my closeness to my sister is?"

He squinted at her, bringing out the crinkles at the

sides of his eyes. Were they brown? No, they were green, she realized. A deep leaf green.

"I thought you wanted to help find the person responsible for your sister's death."

Molly drew in a deep breath. She did. That was the whole reason she was there.

Appetizers were served and Alan chatted with the waiter for a couple of moments, talking about what had been brought in this morning. After the young man left, Chevalier motioned for her to help herself.

"It's meant to be shared," he said.

She accepted a small plate on which he'd placed two of the thick shrimp scampi—or did they call them something else down here?

"I have three sisters," he said, looking at his food rather than her as he spoke. "All younger. And I couldn't tell you much about what's going on in their lives, either."

Molly felt as though he'd just pressed a thumb against a low pressure point, releasing the tension there.

She smiled easily. "Thanks."

He shrugged, considering her warily. "Don't mention it." He ate for a couple moments, then asked, "So when do you go home?"

Suddenly Molly stiffened again, because it was obvious he'd meant as in today or tomorrow, the day after tomorrow at the latest.

He leaned closer to her, his expression intense. "Look, Miss Laraway, I know your intentions are good, but the fact is, there's nothing you can do down here. You might as well go back home and resume your life. Nothing you can do can bring your sister back."

Molly leaned forward, as well. "Tell me, Detective Chevalier, how many unsolved homicide cases do you have open at any one time?"

His eyes narrowed.

She picked up her purse and took out a photograph. "This is a picture of me and my sister taken at our college graduation." She put it on the table in front of him. "Look at it."

"Miss Laraway—"

"Look at it," she repeated.

He sighed and picked up the shot.

"My twin, my sister, was a living, breathing human being, not just a crime victim."

He tried to hand the picture back.

"No, you keep it. Put it on top of the countless ones you probably have of her postmortem." She crossed her arms. "The sooner you accept that I'm not going anywhere, Detective, the sooner we can push aside all the BS and get down to the business of catching this killer before he takes the life of someone else's sister." She swallowed hard. "And before you have someone else like me to deal with."

He seemed unfazed by her words, looking at her much the way he had when he'd first sat down at the table.

Molly searched for more arguments with which

she might convince him. "I'm a lawyer, Detective. Familiar with the law. Use me. I can do legwork you might not have time for. Investigate far-fetched angles you've already ruled out that might still be viable. Make sure you're not without a cup of coffee at all times."

"You're personally attached to the case," he said.

"Which means I'm doubly committed to seeing the job gets done."

He leaned back in his chair. "Coffee, huh?"

His lopsided smile made her retract a few claws. But just a few. Because she had the feeling that if he did take her on, he'd send her out for coffee...permanently.

Still, her options were few. "If that's what it takes to be included in the investigation...yes."

"Well, then," he said quietly, "while department policy prevents anything official, it looks like you've got yourself a job."

Her pulse leaped.

"But let's get a few things straight. I define the job as we go along. I'm the boss and you're the subordinate. And you cannot tell anyone else about this, ever. Do anything I tell you not to and our little arrangement ends. Do I make myself clear?"

She nodded, incapable of words.

"Good, then." He grinned, although his eyes remained watchful. "My first order is that we enjoy this meal before we get down to the gritty details...."

# 3

I STOOD ON THE CURB outside Tujague's and watched Molly Laraway walk toward the nearest intersection, her jacket folded over her arm as she hailed a cab. The woman was a stunner, that was for sure. She had a swing to her walk that caught not only my attention but the eye of every breathing male within a two-block radius.

I stared at the guy next to me watching Molly in the same way I was, then grimaced and patted my front shirt pocket, even though what I was looking for wasn't there and hadn't been there for years: cigarettes.

Truth was, I wasn't sold on the idea of having a loose cannon like Molly running around doing Lord only knew what. But I admired her spirit. And I had the feeling that no matter what I said or did or threatened her with, she would go ahead with her own investigation into her sister's death. Might as well try to channel some of that energy to my own advantage…and keep her safe at the same time.

I patted my coat pockets and took out my cell phone. By directing her actions, I could keep her away from anything remotely dangerous. Not that I thought she was in danger, but at this point I wasn't taking any chances.

And if working with her also kept her in close physical proximity, where I could continue to admire those great legs and possibly charm my way between them…well, I wasn't complaining.

I pressed the auto dial for Steven Chan.

"Tell me you're not calling about this morning's body," he said by way of hello.

"It was worth a try."

"I haven't even unpacked the samples yet."

"Yeah, well, do it. I need the results yesterday."

I closed the phone and walked in the opposite direction from where Molly had gone.

MOLLY CHECKED THE address on her notepad. A modified pickup truck sat in front of the place in question, and a guy was carrying a box out and putting it in the truck bed.

"Excuse me," she said, approaching him as she tucked the pad back into her bag. "I was wondering if you could tell me where I could find Joann Bennett?"

The guy stared at her. "What's it to you?"

"I'm Molly Laraway, Claire Laraway's sister."

Since he didn't seem to recognize her, she suspected that he'd never met her twin.

"Oh, yeah. Joann's ex-roommate. You'll find her inside."

Molly looked over the items already crammed into the back of the truck. "Thanks."

She stepped over the curb and nearer to the door, knocking on the jamb when she found the door was open.

"Miss Bennett?" she called out.

A woman carrying another box came out of what looked like a bedroom, the small living room before her empty of furniture. She looked at Molly, then put the box on top of another one, flushed from her activities. "Are you here to see the apartment?" she asked, pushing her hair back. Then she seemed to get a closer look at Molly and her face went white.

"I'm Claire's twin," Molly said quickly. "I was hoping you might have a couple of minutes."

"Jesus, for a minute I thought you were her."

"I've been getting that a lot lately." She moved out of the way of the guy, who was coming back inside. "I won't keep you long, I promise. I just wanted to ask a couple of questions."

Joann looked at the man, who shrugged. "Sure. Why not?" She sighed. "I'd offer you something to drink, but I've already cleared out the kitchen."

"Moving?" Molly stated the obvious.

"Yes. I was having a hard time finding another roommate and, well—" she lifted her left hand "—my boyfriend proposed."

Molly smiled. "Congratulations."

"Thanks."

She moved aside again as the guy—apparently the fiancé—hefted another box and made his way back outside. "I'm sure Claire would have been happy for you."

"I don't know about that. Claire never met Nick."

"So you two didn't spend a lot of time here?"

"More like Claire didn't spend a lot of time here. Do you mind if I work while we talk?"

"No. Go ahead." Molly moved nearer to the door she'd disappeared into. "So you and my sister weren't close?"

"No, unfortunately, we weren't." Joann wrapped a ceramic knickknack and placed it in an open box. "Truth is, we never got much of a chance to get to know each other well. She only moved in two months before she...died."

Molly remembered her mother giving her the change of address, although she'd never had cause to use it herself.

"Isn't that dangerous?" she asked. "Living with someone you don't know well?"

Joann shrugged as she wrapped another item. "I've had at least seven roommates throughout college up until now. I've never run into any problems. Well, not many, anyway, you know, beyond loud nighttime activities and a piece of jewelry or designer clothing going missing. But even that didn't happen often." She began closing the box. "It's hard to make the rent as a single nowadays, as you may know."

Actually, Molly didn't know. Straight out of high school she'd interned at a law office that had hired her part-time. Then in college she'd become a P.A. and later assistant to a local appellate-court judge. She'd never been rolling in money, but she'd never had a problem making the rent. And she'd always been single.

Joann passed her with the box she'd been carrying when Molly had arrived. "Would you like me to bring this one?" she asked.

"Sure. Thanks."

Molly picked up the other box and followed her out into the living room, where Nick took the carton out of her hands and disappeared outside again.

"You wouldn't happen to have come across anything more of my sister's while you were packing, would you?" She adjusted her purse still slung over her shoulder.

"Funny you should mention that." Joann put down the box and walked into the kitchen. A moment later she came back with a key on a ring that held a pink-haired troll with a blue ink stripe across its face. Molly immediately recognized it as belonging to Claire. She'd bought it to top off a Christmas gift years ago, and her sister had lamented that she'd put a pen mark on it during a phone conversation shortly thereafter.

Molly hadn't paid much attention. Until now.

She took the key.

"I don't know what it opens. Not the apartment. I already tried. And Claire didn't have a car."

"Maybe it's to the place she lived before?"

Joann shrugged. "Maybe. But Nick thought it looked more like a locker key—you know, like the type you see at the bus station? Only it doesn't have a number on it or anything."

Molly ran her thumb over the top of the key, noticing where a line of jagged orange plastic seemed to indicate something had been removed. Nothing but the name of a popular key company was imprinted on the key itself.

"Is there maybe something you've remembered since Claire died?" Molly asked. "Something you haven't told the police?"

"No. I've told them everything I know."

Nick came back inside for the last box. "You ready?" he asked Joann.

"Yeah, give me a sec to double-check."

Molly stood exchanging glances with Nick as cupboard doors were opened and closed in the kitchen, then in the bathroom. Within moments Joann was back in the living room.

"That's it."

"Lock up. I'll be in the truck." Nick disappeared again for a final time.

The key bit into Molly's hand where she held it so tightly.

"Hey, look," Joann said. "I'm really sorry for your loss. I mean, what happened to Claire..." She crossed her arms and rubbed her hands over the bumps that dotted her skin. "I can't imagine what you must be going through right now."

"Thanks."

Joann began to pass her.

"Would you mind if I asked for your forwarding address? In case I have any other questions?" Molly asked.

Joann looked hesitant.

"I promise I won't call unless I'm absolutely convinced you can be of help. In fact, chances are you'll never hear from me again."

Molly pulled her pad and a pen from her purse. And, after a sigh, Joann took it and scribbled down an address and a phone number.

"Thanks," Molly said again, unsure how any of this helped her but glad that she'd caught Joann before she'd left.

Molly led the way outside, then stood watching as Joann climbed into the truck cab, gave a final wave and drove away.

THE GOOD THING ABOUT being a homicide detective was that you didn't spend a lot of time at the office. The bad thing about being a homicide detective was that when you did need to be at the office, you were at a desk in a room shared by a dozen others.

Phones rang, voices chattered, computer printers printed. And one of the younger narc detectives was even trying to figure out how to use the manual typewriter in the corner—and not having much luck, judging by the occasional string of profanities he muttered.

At least I was no longer the center of attention. Ten months ago I couldn't walk into a precinct room without it going completely silent, everyone staring at me.

I guess that was what happened when you bedded the captain's estranged wife.

While few incidents could trump the losing card I'd dealt myself with that stupid move, the more time passed, the more people moved on with their own lives, leaving me alone to see to the ugly details on my own. Although I'm sure an office pool was running to see when the captain would finally fire my sorry ass.

And that day would be soon if I didn't catch a break in the Quarter Killer case.

I edged my chair closer to my paperwork-covered desk and leafed through the mess that threatened to topple over into my lap. Actually, it appeared to have slid onto the floor and been piled back up by someone, because it was messier than usual. I sighed and started sorting through it, knowing it was too much to hope that somewhere in there I would find the clue I needed to solve the Laraway and Arkart murders.

The phone on the corner rang. I ignored it.

"Chevalier, line two for you," a junior detective called out.

"Take a message."

"Take your own damn message. What, do I look like your secretary?"

I glared at him, wondering when he'd grown a pair of balls when only a short time ago he'd been all about pleasing everyone, then snatched up the receiver.

"What?"

"Alan?"

A female voice. More specifically, a female voice belonging to the oldest of my three sisters, Emilie.

I took a deep breath. "Now's not really a good time, Em. Can I call you back?"

"Normally I would say yes, but what I have to say really shouldn't wait."

I rubbed my forehead, wishing for a cup of coffee. "What is it?"

"Zoe hasn't been back to her dorm room in two days."

My hand froze.

Zoe was the youngest of the Chevalier family, although at twenty-one she liked to pretend otherwise. Em and Laure had long ago tried to convince me that they were overcompensating for the loss of their parents by spoiling her, but neither of them had seemed capable of doing anything differently. After all, Zoe had only been eleven at the time, and while they both had their own ghosts to wrestle with, it seemed easier to focus their attention on their youngest sibling than address their own needs.

"How do you know this?" I asked.

"I talked to her roommate."

"Does the roommate have any idea where she might have gone?"

"Not a clue. Her overnight bag is still there and nothing seems to be missing."

Another junior detective called out. "Chevalier? Call on line four."

I gritted my teeth.

Emilie said, "That's not like Zoe at all. She usually lets everyone know where she is and what her plans are. Including me."

She was right. From a young age, all of us had drilled into Zoe the importance of keeping in contact at all times. And she'd complied. Probably because the one time she hadn't, when she was fifteen and had gone to the movies with a male friend, she'd found half the NOPD drawing guns on her in the middle of the theater.

"I'll stop by sometime this afternoon," I told Em, then rang off.

I grabbed my hat and started to get up, half relieved that I wouldn't have to tackle my desk just then.

"You still have that call waiting on four," the junior detective shouted.

I picked up the receiver again and punched the button for line four. "What?"

No one said anything.

Good. They'd hung up.

"Alan?"

Another female voice. But this time it didn't belong to one of my sisters. It belonged to a person I'd never expected—scratch that, never wanted—to hear from again.

Captain Seymour Hodge's wife, Astrid.

# 4

THE WOMAN WAS A certifiable nutcase.

And as much as I wanted to hang up the phone, I couldn't, because essentially she had my nuts in a case.

"Um, hello. How are you?" I said lamely.

I looked around the room, but no one seemed to notice my sudden distress. I sat back down in my chair, the paperwork on my desk nothing but a blur as I tried to recall what had motivated me to get involved with this woman, who had caused far more trouble than she'd been worth.

"I'm sorry, Alan. I didn't mean to call, but I had to."

I opened my desk drawer, looking for aspirin to quell the headache that had been with me since I'd gotten up that morning and that had just doubled in size.

"I mean," Astrid continued, "I just wanted to see how you were doing."

"I thought we both agreed that further contact wouldn't be wise." My exact words the last time we spoke had been *Talking to you again would be akin to professional suicide,* but I didn't like thinking the words, much less saying them again.

"I want to see you."

"Impossible."

"I'll keep calling until you come over."

I winced. "So call."

Then I did something I also didn't think was wise and hung up.

MOLLY SAT IN THE MIDDLE of her hotel-room bed. She'd showered and had on the hotel robe, her hair up in a towel, even though it was only six o'clock. The contents of the box of things she'd gotten from FBI agent Akela Brooks were spread out in front of her, her sister's diary the focal point. But try as she might, she couldn't seem to concentrate. Instead her gaze kept going to the key in her hand, and her mind kept retracing a path to her lunch with Alan Chevalier earlier.

She'd wanted to call him, tell him of her find. But they'd already agreed to meet at a nearby bar on Bourbon Street tomorrow night to trade any information either of them had come across, even though she had a pretty good idea she'd be the only one trading anything. She supposed it could wait until then.

Besides, she knew the instant she told him about the key he'd take it, and she'd likely never see it again, much less find out what was in the box it opened.

Of course, she actually had to find the box first if she hoped to learn anything, an impossible task given her outsider status in the investigation. Bus station aside, she wouldn't know where to begin looking.

After all, there was the little matter of the number that had been removed from the key.

How many lockers were at the bus station? Was there only one station or were there several? Did the airport have lockers? Could it be there?

"For all I know, the box could be in Toledo," she said aloud.

She stretched out her arm and put the key on the nightstand, then rubbed the arch of her left foot. Lunch aside, she'd been pretty much upright all day, pounding the pavement in shoes that were made for walking but not to the extent she had walked in them. She had blisters on her heels, and her toes looked swollen to twice their normal size. So on the way back to the hotel she'd stopped inside a shop and bought comfortable flats, a couple of pairs of casual slacks and lighter-weight blouses, a wardrobe more conducive to the type of work she'd be doing in the days to come.

She'd also bought a flirty dress that she had no business buying. A deep-red number that looked more like a slip than a dress, really, and felt like a cloud against her bare skin—and left a lot of that skin bare to the naked eye.

It had to be the city. She'd never been one to dress so provocatively—not even when she was younger—much less give herself over to such an impulsive buy. She'd always been practical to the max.

No, the purchase would have been much more something Claire would have made, even if it meant maxing out a credit card. "Retail therapy," she'd called it.

Molly had called it stupid. If you didn't have the cash, you didn't need the buy.

Molly certainly didn't need the dress, yet she'd gone ahead and bought it anyway. Perhaps with thoughts of seeing the look on Alan's face when she wore it.

She sighed and slid from the bed. What was she talking about? She wasn't interested in the burned-out detective. She was the girl next door; he had a dark, edgy side. He appeared to have little ambition beyond what he was going to eat that day; she had a list of fifty things she hoped to accomplish before she was thirty and was aware of that list at all times. She put attraction and physical chemistry on the back burner; he put it out there for anyone to see, no matter the consequences.

Molly swallowed thickly. That was what she was really responding to, wasn't it? The fundamental call of attraction. It had been there in his eyes as he'd sat across from her. No need for words, for his movements and expressions spoke for him.

She absently tidied up the room. She wasn't used to that. That…knowing. More often than not she was genuinely surprised to find a man interested in her. Oh, not so much because she didn't think she was attractive. But because in the Midwest, men—people in general, really—tended to keep their true emotions in check. Perhaps it was tied into pride. Or maybe she just wasn't really good at reading emotions because she'd spent so little time contemplating her own.

But today had shown her that she didn't need a degree in sociology and human behavior to know Alan Chevalier had been attracted to her.

Or that she had been just as attracted to him.

What remained was whether or not she acted on it. Because another thing Alan had made plainly clear was that she held all the cards. It was up to her to ante up or to fold and walk away from the table. He would not force her hand. Would not sandbag or bluff or try anything underhanded to get her to do what he wanted.

No. In his case, what you saw was what you got.

And Molly found something undeniably appealing about that. She really hadn't encountered it since her sister. Whatever Claire had been thinking, feeling, you knew it the instant she did. While Molly didn't believe in any sort of paranormal connection to her twin, they had been closely connected. Partly because of the emotional unavailability of their mother, who'd gone through her share of pain in her lifetime—the first and foremost her unexpected pregnancy with them when she'd still been in high school and no support system of her own when her family members had turned their backs on her.

While later on they'd grown apart, she and Claire had been tighter than tight while growing up.

And she was seeing the same potential in her attraction for Alan. She sensed the possibility for a connection that went beyond the physical.

And her need to explore that possibility loomed almost as large as her desire to find her sister's killer.

OF ALL MY ACCOMPLISHMENTS, I counted my sisters as the most important.

Of all my failures, my sisters ranked number one by a long shot.

Years ago the department shrink told me that was to be expected. Most parents experienced mixed feelings when it came to their children. Both of us had known at the time that my family situation wasn't supposed to be the topic of conversation; rather my shooting of a minor holding what had looked like a handgun but had turned out to be a water pistol was. But her psychological digging had turned up the conflicts I'd been facing at home.

Both of us had also known I wasn't any kind of parent, either, although it was the role I'd been forced to take ten years ago, when I was twenty-six and my sisters were sixteen, thirteen and eleven. When my father had been targeted by carjackers and had decided his secondhand Mercedes was more important than his life and his wife's, my stepmother's. The incident was what had inspired me to become a homicide detective rather than a beat cop.

It was also what had made me the unprepared parent to two teenagers and a preteen.

My father's family was among the first to settle here when my great-great-grandfather was assigned a judgeship by none other than Jefferson himself back in the early 1800s. With ancestors who were among the first important founders of the city, my father felt our family bore a certain responsibility. But his take was one I'd never really subscribed to. Probably because my own mother had been of questionable heritage (read: she'd been a stripper on Bourbon Street when my father had met her) and had thrown his unnamed title into his face when she'd left us both when I was four.

So when my father and his wife had died, I'd moved back into the mammoth house that had been in my family since my ancestors had moved down to Louisiana from the Boston area, and tried my best to be a surrogate parent to my three younger sisters.

It was that same house I now stood in front of, experiencing myriad mixed feelings.

Emilie and Laure still lived there. It was where Emilie had gotten married two years ago and now had a child of her own. A house that Zoe hadn't seemed to be able to get out of fast enough when she was eighteen and moved to a dorm on the campus of Tulane. I rubbed the back of my neck, marveling at how similar her actions had been to my own so long ago. Before I was forced back into that house and into the role of "guardian."

"Thank God you're here," Emilie said, opening

the door at my first knock. "I still haven't heard anything from Zoe. She's not answering her cell phone, and Laure hasn't had any luck getting anything out of her friends."

It also appeared Emilie was having problems in other areas as she bounced one-year-old Henri on her hip, the toddler's face red and damp from tears.

She led the way back to the kitchen, where they had always spent a great deal of their time. There, Emilie's young husband, James, was making what looked like dinner by way of sandwiches, and Laure was on the phone, apparently talking to another of Zoe's friends.

I put my hat on the rectangular table that sat six and shrugged out of my overcoat, taking Henri when Emilie thrust him at me.

"He's teething," she said.

I went to the sink and placed the toddler on the counter next to me while I washed my hands, then picked him back up.

"Is there some way you can trace her cell?" Laure asked, disconnecting from her call.

"Only if she answers it," I told her.

Henri had taken to chomping on my index finger. I winced, discovering that a tooth or two or three had already broken through his tender gums and were now breaking into my flesh.

Out of the three girls, Zoe was the one most capable of taking care of herself.

And the other two had been old enough when their parents had died that the trauma of losing loved ones had never completely left them.

Suddenly every eye was on me, including the two big blues of the baby in my arms.

"What?"

Laure waved her hand. "What what? What have you done since Emilie called this morning?"

I raised my eyebrows. I hadn't done anything. "I was waiting until I came over here for details."

"You already have all the details," Emilie said, taking Henri away from me as if he'd been a gift she was now rescinding.

I shared a look with James, who immediately went back to making sandwiches that for all intents and purposes had been done five minutes ago.

"So what are you going to do? Have you put an APB out on her? Have you gone to the dorm?"

"I'm guessing you already have," I said.

"Of course *we* have. But we don't have badges."

"I don't think Zoe would appreciate my flashing my badge around campus."

"I don't care what Zoe appreciates—and that's assuming everything's okay."

Laure shuddered and wrapped her arms around her slender torso.

"Look," I said, picking up a piece of salami and putting it into my mouth, "this isn't the first time Zoe's pulled something like this."

Actually, it wasn't the second or third, either, but I wasn't going to point that out. To do so would be to hurt Emilie and Laure by trivializing their concern, and I wasn't prepared to do that.

"Two days isn't all that long a period of time."

"But what if she's been kidnapped?" Emilie asked.

Her fear must have manifested itself physically, because Henri suddenly started crying.

James took him and mumbled something about changing his diaper as he disappeared from the room. Neither of my sisters appeared to notice.

"If she'd been kidnapped, then surely a ransom demand would have been made by now."

As if on cue, the phone rang, echoing eerily throughout the silent house.

Laure and Emilie raced for it, while I put the top on one of the sandwiches and took a bite. Hey, I hadn't eaten since lunch and I was hungry.

"Hello?" Laure said, winning the race.

Her tensed shoulders relaxed as she listened to someone who was apparently not a kidnapper.

"Hi, Rose. No, no word yet. I want to keep the line open in case…she calls. I'll let you know the minute we hear anything."

She hung up again and looked back to me.

There were few things that could floor me. But the two women staring at me as if waiting for me to pull answers out of my sleeves like a magician's never-ending scarf was one of them.

"All right, I'll look into it," I said under my breath.

Emilie hugged me, and Laure looked more relieved than I felt comfortable witnessing.

Was it really only yesterday I'd been helping Laure with her homework while Emilie had braided Zoe's hair in this very kitchen, a pot of gumbo on the stove while the radio played tinny zydeco or jazz?

Yesterday and ten years ago.

"Thanks, Al," Emilie murmured, her cheek soft against my stubble-covered one.

"Not that I think it's going to accomplish anything. Watch and see if our renegade little sister doesn't call herself before I can find out anything."

"We can only hope that's the case," Laure said.

The telephone rang again. James walked back into the room with a still-wailing Henri, and Emilie went to put the sandwiches on plates.

Laure picked up the phone. "Oh, hi, Valerie. No, no word yet. Yes, yes, he's here now."

My ex-wife.

I dry-washed my face to hide my frown from Em. "You called Valerie?"

"Don't look so surprised," she said from the other side of the counter. "Even though you two are divorced, Val's still like family to us."

"No, not yet," Laure was saying. "We're going to call around to the hospitals now."

An image of my father's slack face where he'd

lain in a curtained-off area of the hospital emergency room flashed through my mind.

And for the first time I knew a fear that my sisters' concerns might be warranted.

# 5

"It appears you have significant contacts, Miss Laraway."

Molly wasn't sure if the smile prosecutor Bill Grissom was giving her was genuine, but she was certain his words were. She'd spent the better part of the morning on the phone with the Toledo law office where she worked, probing who knew whom and what help their extended circle of professional acquaintances could offer her. She'd lucked out when it turned out a junior partner's wife's family was from New Orleans and her father-in-law was a prominent judge in Jefferson Parish.

A few more phone calls later and she was standing in the prosecutor's office, shaking hands with him.

"Do you have any suggestions on what I might send Judge Giroux by way of thanks?"

Grissom chuckled. "A good bottle of bourbon should do the trick. In fact, a case wouldn't be turned away."

"Thank you. I'll keep that in mind."

"Please, have a seat."

She did, and then he rounded his desk and sat down, as well.

"So what can I do to help you, Miss Laraway?"

"I need to know what information you have on my sister's murder case."

He clasped his hands tightly on the desk before him. "Ah, yes. I was afraid when I heard your last name that's what you would be interested in." He shook his head. "I'm sorry, but even if you were related to the president of the United States, I couldn't share information like that with you."

Molly frowned. "Mr. Grissom, I assure you that I'm not on a vigilante mission. I'm merely interested in seeing that my sister's killer is brought to justice."

He returned her stare.

"I understand that a Claude Lafitte was originally arrested for the crime."

"Yes. And he was promptly released."

"Why?"

He smiled patiently. "Because we ascertained that he couldn't have committed the crime."

"And the evidence that supports that?"

"Is in my file."

"Does that mean there's another suspect under investigation?" Molly held her breath as she considered the possibility.

"Not per se. Let's just say that the evidence pointed us in a different direction."

"But you don't have any one person under consideration."

"Not at the moment, no." He gripped his chair arms and sat back. "I understand you've been in contact with the detective in charge of the case."

"Alan Chevalier. Yes."

He nodded. "And he's being accommodating?"

"In a manner of speaking, yes."

His expression registered brief surprise. "Well, then, he'd be more the man to talk to. Whatever happens goes through him before reaching this office. And until we do get that one suspect..."

"I understand," she said, rising. "I just thought it would be a good idea to touch base with you. Let you know I was in town and willing to help in any capacity I can."

"I appreciate the gesture."

She shook his hand again. "And I appreciate your hospitality. Thank you for meeting with me."

Molly walked out of the office and released a long sigh. She'd suspected that meeting with the prosecutor wouldn't yield much. But surprisingly it had given her more than Alan had. So Claude Lafitte had been released because evidence had pointed in another direction. What evidence? And in which direction did it point?

She'd put on her suit for the meeting and decided to make a trip back to the hotel to change. Which would also give her the opportunity to call FBI agent

Akela Brooks. Perhaps she could get the answers to those two questions before meeting Alan tonight at the bar on Bourbon Street.

"DETECTIVE CHEVALIER? I have another emergency call for you. I'll patch it through."

I nearly snapped the cell phone in two.

This was the sixth call I'd received in three hours. It seemed Astrid was keeping her promise to keep calling me until I agreed to stop by and see her. During my last brief, tense conversation with her, she'd said she wouldn't try anything; she just needed to see me.

Somehow I didn't believe her.

I quickened my step as I walked from the precinct to my car and climbed inside. At least she hadn't told dispatch who she was. I could be thankful for at least that much. But there was no telling how long that would last. Astrid Hodge was a woman used to getting what she wanted. And for some godforsaken reason she wanted me.

"Hello, Alan." Her voice came through the tinny speaker dripping with self-satisfaction.

My every bone tensed.

"You know, your calls can be traced via your home number," I said. "What's your husband going to say when he sees the bill?"

"I'm calling on my personal cell. And he doesn't have access to the bill."

Which made her intent doubly suspicious.

"When are you stopping by, Alan?"

"Never. I value my job too much."

She made a tsking sound. "More than me."

"Much more than you."

"That hurts."

"Not any more than you've hurt me over the past ten months."

"We both know that what happened between us was mutual."

Was it? I was no longer sure. I mean, for all intents and purposes, I'd believed that in the beginning. But as time wore on, and after she'd accidentally told her husband—my captain—about our affair of one night, I was beginning to wonder if I'd fallen into some sort of dark trap designed to help Astrid spice up her marriage.

"Give it up, Astrid. I'm not coming over."

She started to say something, but I clicked the phone shut on her.

I sat for long moments in the car, staring at everything and nothing. All I could do was hope that she'd finally give up and stop calling. But a part of me knew that she wouldn't. That eventually she would win and I would have to go over to her place.

The sex hadn't even been that good.

I put the car into gear and pulled from the curb, my destination Hotel Josephine. I'd received an anonymous tip that the hotel's only guest wasn't who he claimed to be. While the owner, Josie Villefranche, had told me Drew Morrison was in town for a convention, it turned out her guest's intentions weren't quite that innocent. A few calls had verified that while he was registered at the Innovation in Auto Parts convention at the Marriott, his area of expertise wasn't car engines; it was in getting people to sell what they didn't want to. Namely he was there to convince Josie to sell her hotel.

While it didn't make him suspect material—especially since the Quarter Killer's first victim, Molly's twin sister, had been killed more than two weeks ago—it did shine a poor light on him. And it was worth checking out if only to see what else Mr. Morrison might be lying about.

The cell I'd dropped into my lap chirped again. I hated these damn devices. There was a time not too long ago that you could escape the telephone. When you walked away from the office, you were out of contact. Period.

At the very least, couldn't they make the damn things sound like a real phone?

"What?" I barked after fumbling to answer it.

"Alan?"

My ex-wife.

MOLLY MADE ARRANGEMENTS to meet with FBI agent Akela Brooks in Jackson Square at three. It was a week before Halloween, and she guessed that this time of year was a busy one for the city, second only to Mardi Gras for pulling in visitors. People clogged the tourist attractions, signs all over touting the weeklong All Hallow's Eve festivities beginning tonight. A group of five individuals of about her age brushed past her dressed in full-out vampire gear, their faces painted white, their black capes flapping in their wake.

Molly gave a shiver.

"Takes all kinds, doesn't it?"

She turned at the sound of Akela's voice. She'd met the agent when she'd picked up the box of her sister's things upon her arrival. While the meeting had been brief, Molly had liked her. She was direct, no-nonsense and friendly. And the fact that she'd held on to Claire's things even though their mother hadn't wanted them to be forwarded to her spoke volumes.

"Thanks for coming."

"Sure." Akela looked over her shoulder toward the Café Du Monde. "You want to get some coffee and walk while we talk?"

Molly agreed, and after they stood in line at the popular spot, Akela handed her a coffee and a sugar-covered beignet.

"You can't come to New Orleans and not try the Café Du Monde beignets," she told her.

Molly smiled and accepted both.

"So, what's on your mind?" Akela didn't waste any time getting to the point as they walked across the square.

"I met with the prosecutor this morning."

"Ah, Grissom."

"Yes. And he mentioned something about Claude Lafitte being released from custody as the result of specific evidence pointing in another direction."

Akela looked at her as she ate her own beignet and sipped her coffee. She didn't say anything.

"I also understand you have a personal interest in the case."

The agent sighed. "Well, I guess that wouldn't be too hard to find out."

Molly pinched off a piece of the French doughnut and put it into her mouth, not answering until she'd swallowed. "You're right. It wasn't difficult. All I had to do was access the *Times-Picayune* between the time of my sister's death and now."

Akela nodded. "Yes, I do have a personal interest," she said. "Let's just say that I'm as interested in finding the Quarter Killer as the NOPD. More so, actually."

"Are you working the case?"

"In an unofficial capacity, yes. You see, until the real killer is found, Claude won't be completely ruled out as a suspect."

"So the evidence pointing in another direction isn't that strong."

"Strong enough to get the department to release him but not enough to completely take him off the suspect list."

"I see." Molly squinted at her through a shaft of

sunlight. "You wouldn't happen to want to share that piece of evidence, would you?"

Akela made a face. "I don't like playing coy, but right now that evidence is about my only ace in the hole." She cleaned her hands with her napkin after finishing her beignet. "You do know there's been another Quarter killing, don't you?"

The coffee sliding down Molly's throat turned bitter.

"It's all over the morning papers and the news on TV."

She'd been so busy, she hadn't thought to read the newspaper or watch local television since her arrival. Especially since she was in the middle of chasing down leads in her sister's case.

But if there'd been another murder, that might mean more evidence.

"Yes, Chevalier questioned Claude on it this morning. But I got the impression the action was somehow just his covering all the bases."

"How so?"

"I don't know. I think he doesn't necessarily believe the two murders are connected, even though they took place at the same hotel and, apparently, in the same way."

"The victim's neck…"

"Was cut," Akela finished when Molly didn't.

"When?"

"Yesterday morning."

Yesterday morning. That meant that Alan had

known about the killing before he'd met with her for lunch. The coffee hit her stomach like a stone. She'd known that she couldn't rely on his sharing everything with her, but concealing that there had been another murder went beyond the mere protection of important facts.

Or was Akela right in that he didn't believe the two murders were linked?

Whatever the reason, she fully expected him to share what he knew when she met up with him tonight. And she would do everything in her power to see that he did.

# 6

DREW MORRISON, THE ONLY guest at Hotel Josephine, didn't have anything to do with Frederique Arkart's killing, of that much I was sure. But right now everything was up for grabs. Because ruling out Morrison didn't change the fact that I had two dead women on my hands and zero solid suspects.

I drove through the narrow streets of the Quarter, heading in a direction I didn't want to be heading as I checked my cell phone. I typically leave it in the car when I'm questioning a potential suspect or witness because there are few things like a shrill chirp and an unwanted caller to throw me off my game and put me back to square one when it comes to any kind of rhythm in my questioning tactics.

There was an art to getting what I wanted out of someone. A certain way of phrasing a question, pausing for just the right amount of time, that netted me information I wouldn't get otherwise. I had taken great pride in that talent at one time.

But now I seemed to be just going through the motions, more aware of the shadows lurking behind me, trying to catch up and pull me into the darkness, than what lay in front of me.

Two messages from the precinct indicating emergency calls had come in while I'd been at the Josephine. Astrid, it had to be. My sisters had my cell phone number, so there was no reason for them to go through dispatch. I stopped at an intersection and scrolled through the calls. My ex-wife's number popped up and I winced. Probably she was calling about Zoe again.

Throwing the phone to the other side of the bench seat, I continued driving. It wasn't that I harbored any ill feelings toward Valerie. For all intents and purposes, me and my ex got along well. Val liked to say it was because I hadn't been emotionally invested in our relationship from the beginning. I'd never gotten into pop psych, so I couldn't tell you if that was the case. But she made a very compelling argument.

*Alan, admit it—you married me to provide a mother for your sisters,* she said.

Of course, I hadn't admitted it. Because to do so I would be classifying myself as a jerk of the highest order. I mean, who married someone for reasons having to do with anything other than love?

While I hadn't admitted it to her, I was grudgingly coming to realize that she might have been right.

Oh, Valerie was a looker. Tall. Brunette. Sexy as hell. And she had a generous streak a mile wide. She'd taken to the girls the first time she'd come by the house to meet me for a date. Since I'd had so much on my plate at the time, I hadn't actively pursued her; rather she'd pursued me. And she had comfortably invaded every facet of my life as easily as a woman's sweet perfume filled a room.

*It's not your fault, Alan,* she'd told me when I'd come home five years into our marriage to find her packing. *I'm the one who charged into this with my eyes wide open. It's just...I don't know. I thought that somewhere along the way this would turn into a real marriage and that we would start creating a family of our own.*

But I hadn't been open to a discussion relating to kids. Hadn't I had enough on my hands with three parentless sisters who at the time had needed full-time attention?

Of course, the task had become monumentally easier with Valerie's involvement. She'd played the role of surrogate mother to a tee, supplying guidance and compassion along with packed lunches and allowing me to focus more on my increasingly demanding career.

But the girls had grown up and begun living lives of their own, shining a harsh spotlight on the fact that the life Valerie and I had shared had been more about the girls than us.

And the bond she had formed with my sisters had been much stronger than any bond we'd had between us. Evidenced by the fact that Emilie had called her, perhaps even before calling me, to share that Zoe had gone missing.

A man in a wrinkled overcoat stumbled out into the street in front of the car. I jammed on the brakes just in time to keep from making him a hood ornament. He looked at me and I stared back. He was maybe ten years older than I was and his eyes were bloodshot; he was clearly drunk. It struck me, sitting there in my car, that I could have been looking at a mirror image of myself down the road.

He hit the hood. "Damn it, watch where in the hell you're going, dumbass."

I blinked, shaking myself out of my reverie. He moved away in a jagged path back to the sidewalk, mumbling profanities, as I put the car back in gear and continued on. Five minutes later I reached my destination, parked and climbed out of the car wondering what the hell I was doing there. And just what in the hell I was going to do now.

I stood outside the small Hodge house on the edge of the Garden District and tugged at my tie. I prayed that during the past two calls Astrid Hodge hadn't given her name to any of the precinct personnel when she'd claimed a family emergency and asked to be put through to my cell phone. If she had…

The door before me opened slightly. I blinked into the sliver of darkness, trying to make her out.

"Well, hello, Alan," she said quietly, as if I'd just dropped by from out of the blue for a visit instead of been summoned by badgering phone calls. The door opened farther, and she stood leaning against it wearing a sexy pink robe made of some kind of slinky material.

All at once I became aware of why I'd slept with her. She was sexy as hell and had wanted me. That had been all the incentive I'd needed at the time.

Now I brushed by her into the house, my hands stuffed deep into my pockets.

I heard the door close behind me as I scanned the classically decorated house. Although the structure was small, it was ideally located in a wealthy part of town, and the furnishings were a mixture of antiques and upscale pieces befitting the woman who had just let me in.

"Can I get you something to drink?" Astrid asked, a cloud of expensive perfume enveloping me as she made her way into the living room.

She lifted a crystal decanter full of amber liquid and poured a finger into an etched tumbler. I became aware of an all-too-familiar burning in the back of my throat, as if I'd already downed the pricey bourbon.

"No, thank you," I said with some difficulty, clenching the hands in my pockets. "I'd much rather you tell me what you want."

"Suit yourself." She considered the glass she still held out, smiled, then took a sip herself.

A dull pounding began behind my eyes as I caught a whiff of my drink of choice.

While I did what I wanted with my nights—which lately had included countless bottles of the stuff she was now drinking—I'd somehow managed to keep my thirst from intruding when I was on the job.

Of course, it wasn't too long ago that bedding the captain's wife, no matter how estranged, would also have been something I would have avoided.

But all that was water over the dam.

"Do I really need a reason?" she asked, running her tongue over her red-painted lips.

I followed the motion.

Women.

I'd given up trying to figure them out a long time ago. From my mother, who'd run out on me and my father without looking back, to my ex-wife, who I was closer to now than when we'd been married, to my sisters, and now Molly Laraway and her doe-eyed looks, I didn't think I'd ever put together the puzzle that made them up.

Astrid Hodge at one time had probably been a knockout. One of those women that every man would want in his bed at least once. The type that stopped conversation when she entered a room and made men either wish they had worn looser pants or be glad that they had.

Not that she wasn't attractive now. But at five years my senior and with a predilection toward the bourbon she was currently sipping, life had begun taking its toll—something she could hide well at night but that was painfully apparent in the light of day. Rather than smoothing out small imperfections, the makeup she wore seemed to cling to her skin like a mask, her lipstick a little too garish, her eyelids creased with color, her fake eyelashes looking like spiders climbing up her still-attractive face.

She smiled at me, apparently taking my attention the wrong way. "It's good to see you again, Alan."

"I wish I could say the same, Astrid, I really do," I said, not liking that I was standing in the house she again shared with her husband, my immediate superior. "But I'd much rather be standing over a corpse than here."

I knew my words were harsh, but I was in no mood for playing Mr. Nice Guy. It had gotten me into trouble with her before.

Besides, the dull headache behind my eyes was progressing into a pounding migraine.

"Do you have some aspirin?"

"Sure," she said, motioning toward the hall. "In the bathroom upstairs."

I didn't like the thought of going anywhere near the bedroom on the second floor, but the alternative was to allow the pounding in my head to worsen still.

Besides, it would get me away from her for a couple of much-needed minutes.

I climbed the stairs and closed myself in the pink-and-gold lavatory. Little cherubs smiled down at me from the sides of the mirror before I opened the cabinet it concealed. The shelves held the regular household fare: lotions, shaving cream and mouthwash. I picked up a prescription bottle. Ativan. Shocker. I put it back, moved aside K-Y jelly and a case that looked as if it held a diaphragm, then grabbed the bottle of generic aspirin. I emptied a couple of tablets into my palm, then turned on the faucet and washed them down by scooping water into my mouth with my hand rather than using the shiny gold cup in a holder.

For long moments I stood staring at my reflection in the mirror, watching a droplet from the water cling to the stubble on my jaw. I wiped it away and grimaced. While it was all well and good to judge Astrid's waning beauty as somehow lacking, judging my own appearance wasn't something I was up to just then. Partly because I didn't want to think about what my captain's wife saw in me.

Mostly because looking at myself made me think of young and sexy Molly Laraway and how I didn't deserve to look at her, much less encourage the attraction I saw in her big blue eyes.

I swiftly turned from the mirror and made my way back downstairs, relieved that Astrid hadn't followed me and tried to lure me into her bedroom. Ten months ago, her husband had been living out of a hotel downtown because she had booted him out for having an affair. But signs that Hodge was not only back but that the couple was happier than ever—if the picture in the paper of them attending some sort of society function recently was anything to go by—made me decidedly more uncomfortable in this house.

"I've got to go," I said once I reached the hall.

Astrid was leaning against the entryway into the living room. I caught a glimpse of her deep cleavage and the long length of thigh made bare by the way she was standing.

"You're back with your ex-wife, aren't you?" she said, her fingers tightening their grip on the doorway that supported her.

I frowned. What would make her think that? "No, Astrid, I'm not back with Valerie. But you are very clearly back with your husband."

Her gaze went to the splash of amber liquid still in the tumbler. "In a manner of speaking."

What in the hell did she mean by that?

"Goodbye, Astrid. And I hope this will be for the final time."

I stepped outside and pulled the door closed behind me. A moment later I heard the bourbon glass crash against the door.

# 7

I DIDN'T QUITE KNOW WHAT to make of my visit to Astrid's place. I was only glad that I hadn't received another call since I'd stopped by.

I went home to clean up, grabbed a po'boy at the corner restaurant, then walked to the Gas Lantern, where Molly and I had arranged to meet.

As far as bars went, this one wasn't bad. It was far enough away from the Quarter not to be filled with tourists and near enough that it still did a decent bit of business. There really was no decor that I could tell. It was more a dim-the-lights-so-you-couldn't-make-out-the-stain-on-the-floor type of place. But those lights were dimmed just right. And the owner, Jack Cadieux, kept a clean bar, didn't water down his drinks and was fair with prices. I came here often enough that I had a regular table in the corner, where I sat with my back against the wall so I could watch people coming and going. And the minute I sat down, a clean glass and a fresh bottle of bourbon were placed in front of me along with a bowl of hot nuts.

Jack didn't seem to be in on any of the Halloween-week festivities. Which was just fine with me. If I never saw one more native or tourist dressed like a ghoul, it would be too soon.

I loved my city. My connection to it ran through my veins as surely as my Chevalier blood. But I could do without the city-of-the-dead stuff that authors wrote books about and filmmakers made movies about and the tourists hungered to experience, taking the haunted tours and stealing items from local graveyards as keepsakes. A nonstop topic among locals was whether the reality had created the fiction or, as I was prone to believe, the fiction had created the reality.

The Creoles, via Haiti, had indeed brought their voodoo religion to Louisiana, packed in their suitcases along with their underwear. But in my experience, the rituals were harmless and the shops on Bourbon Street little more than fronts to sell voodoo dolls and incense to curious tourists. With a few bizarre exceptions. The other shops, the ones that might be the real deal, lay outside my district and thus outside my interest.

Anyway, that entire aspect…well, that had little to do with the place I knew. The New Orleans I knew was about the thick heat, the spicy food and the jazz. And two centuries of history chock-full of tradition. A tradition my father and my grandfather before him had taken pride in passing on. A tradition that I respected but had shrugged off early on.

A path my youngest sister, Zoe, seemed to also be following, much to my dismay. The first chance she got, she'd moved out of the house to live on campus while attending Tulane, even though the commute between the two was short. She was rebellious and independent and waved off anything having to do with tradition and expectation at every turn, frustrating her older sisters.

Me? Aside from moments like this one, I got a secret little kick out of her antics.

I rubbed my stubble-covered chin and checked my cell phone. No more calls. I wasn't surprised. I'd called Laure to tell her that I had yet to get a line on the baby of the family. She'd likely passed on the news to Emilie. And Valerie, as well, the Chevalier women tight-knit no matter the severing of marital ties.

I'd stopped by Zoe's dorm at Tulane and asked questions earlier in the day. No one seemed to know where she might be, including her roommate, who appeared to have an MP3 player permanently inserted in the side of her head and who looked as blank as a clean sheet of paper.

The Old-Timers, a jazz band that was a regular fixture at Jack's, warmed up in the far corner, the lead singer welcoming the crowd of about twenty-five or so scattered throughout the establishment. I poured a finger of bourbon and turned the glass around and around in front of me. I should have been keeping a clear head, with Molly Laraway still to deal with. But my head pounded despite the aspirin I'd taken at Astrid's, and my mouth watered with the desire to down the fiery shot.

The front door opened and closed as I continued staring at the golden liquid. When I looked up, the new visitor was at the bar, her back to me. I eyed strappy black shoes, then followed the line of her long legs up to the hem of a short dark-red dress that clung to all the right curvy places.

There was a time not too long ago when I might have gone up to the bar and stood beside the new addition, checking out the front as I had the back to see if she was possible one-night-stand material. A little something to provide temporary entertainment, much like the alcohol in front of me. But after the disaster of Astrid, I'd kept pretty much to myself. Besides, the way I looked these days, the woman would more likely move farther down the bar than closer to me.

I stared at my watch, then at the door. Molly was running late. I frowned. She had struck me as the punctual type. Always on time and always with a pad nearby. I took my hat off and put it on the table next to the bourbon, still debating draining the glass's contents.

Jack, who was talking to the new visitor, said something, then pointed in my direction.

The woman in the short dress turned.

Molly Laraway.

Sweet Jesus.

I picked up the glass and downed the contents.

MOLLY WASN'T SURE WHAT she'd expected when she'd walked into the Gas Lantern. Truth was, she'd been a little preoccupied since stepping out of her hotel room in the ultrasexy dress she had on. And it had taken a little concentration to walk in the stiletto heels, higher than anything she'd strapped on before. But Alan's dumbfounded expression made every awkward step worth it.

With a confidence she had in spades in the professional arena—and that she was beginning to acquire in the sexual field—she sauntered over to his table.

"This chair taken?"

He got up so fast he nearly knocked his own chair over.

"Please…sit," he said.

For a minute she thought he might pull her chair out for her. She didn't give him a chance as she smoothed the back of the dress down and seated herself, carefully crossing her legs so as not to give a flash of her panties. There was sexy and there was raunchy. And she wasn't about to cross that line…yet.

Funnily enough, Alan's fumbling response touched off something interesting within her, a power source she had never tapped into before if only because she hadn't known of its existence.

Was that why Claire had dressed the way she had? Had she liked and encouraged the feminine power a mere change in clothing could bring about?

Of course, beyond an irrepressible desire to wear

the impulse purchase—as well as a practical attitude that since she'd spent the money, she should really wear it—she thought the dress might help her convince the detective to reveal more than he wanted to.

She hadn't factored into the equation that his reaction would awaken in her a side of herself she hadn't known existed.

"Can I get you something?" a young waitress asked, balancing an empty tray in her right hand.

Molly eyed the bottle on the table. "Just another glass, please."

"You're late."

She placed her clutch purse next to his hat, resisting the urge to finger the soft brim of the fedora. "I had a little trouble finding the place."

The waitress brought the glass, then left them alone again.

For long moments neither of them said anything. And then Alan seemed to realize that she had an empty glass. He picked up the bottle of bourbon, splashed a portion into her glass, then his. She noticed the way his knuckles whitened where he held it.

He really had great hands. Manly hands. Big and thick-fingered and rough. No, Alan wouldn't know what lotion was, much less use it. It had been a long time since she'd been with a man, and she couldn't remember being with someone with hands so masculine and capable.

She caught the direction of her thoughts. Was she

really contemplating moving beyond the obvious attraction to a sexual liaison with the brooding detective? Yes, she realized, she was. And the acknowledgement sent a heated thrill running over her skin.

"I understand the Quarter Killer has struck again," she said quietly.

Alan grimaced, trying to look everywhere but at her. But time and time again his gaze strayed from the innocuous to what he must have deemed forbidden territory. From his drink to the deep V of her dress. From the bar to her neck, bared by the upswept style she'd tamed her hair into. From the door to her legs, where they stuck out to the left of the small table.

"That's what the media would have you think."

"But it's not the truth?"

The *thump-thump* of the jazz drum seemed to vibrate straight through her as she waited for his response. Though she'd visited a couple of similar bars on Bourbon Street during the day, talking to those who might have seen her sister the night before she'd been killed, this was the first time she'd been in one at night. The dim lights, the smoky room, the band, all combined to create a provocative atmosphere more intoxicating than the bourbon she had yet to touch. She was ultra-aware of the darkening of Alan's eyes as he tried not to look at her but did anyway. The feel of the fabric rubbing against her taut nipples as she crossed and uncrossed her legs. The weightlessness in the pit of her stomach that she could only credit to anticipation. The sudden dryness of her mouth that wouldn't be quenched by her drink.

"No. I don't know." Where she felt inordinately mellow and sensual, Alan seemed about ready to jump out of his skin. "I'm beginning to think the second murder may be a copycat."

It took a moment for Molly to register what he was saying. In fact, every piece of stimuli was taking her more time than usual to process. "That means someone familiar with the details of the first case is the murderer of the prostitute."

He nodded.

"Which means you now have two separate killers on your hands."

"Yeah, that's what it means."

Of course, it also meant there would be zero additional evidence to help them find her sister's killer.

She understood that in any investigation, the first twenty-four hours were the most important. The more time that passed, the odds against finding the killer grew exponentially. Especially if there was no solid evidence to support an investigation.

Silence settled between them again, as if the sensual cloud enveloping her was now including Alan.

"Excuse me," a man said, coming to stand next to their table.

Molly looked up at him as though surprised someone else was in the room.

"Would you like to dance?"

Molly blinked, then glanced toward the area in front of the band. Two couples were indeed dancing to the slower jazz tune.

"Sorry," Alan said, getting up from his chair, dropping a couple of bills onto the table, then picking up his hat. "The lady and I were just leaving."

# 8

I WASN'T ALTOGETHER SURE who was more surprised by my abrupt response to the guy that had asked Molly for a dance—her or me. But I did know that it was something I'd never done before. And that bothered me on a level I wasn't ready to explore.

Okay, so the lady looked great in a dress. Especially this dress. And, all right, *great* didn't begin to cover it. The snug fit and sexy design verified what I could only suspect before: that she was built. Her body was long and shapely, emphasizing the fullness of her pert breasts and hips. And those legs…

I was already aware of my want of her. But her appearance tonight had turned that want into an unfamiliar burning need.

My reaction to the guy asking her for a dance told me something else was at work here. Something strange. The only time I'd essentially told another guy to get lost was when one was stupid enough to approach one of my sisters in my presence. And since Molly wasn't related to me…well, I could only put it down to a need within me to protect her from lechers.

Lechers like me.

"Where are we going?"

I grew aware that I was walking down the street as if a rabid dog was snapping at my heels, and slowed my step. Molly appeared relieved as she halted briefly and leaned against a storefront to adjust one of her decadent sandals. I was overly fascinated with every movement. The way her slender hand rested against the warm brick front. The arch of her neck as she bent to her task. The slide of her index finger as she edged it under the slender strap to straighten it.

I swallowed hard.

Good question. Where were we going?

"I have something else I need to do tonight. I thought we could kill two birds with one stone."

More like I needed to get out of that bar before I either downed the bottle of bourbon or sucker punched the guy, who hadn't been pleased with my response and had told me he'd been speaking to the lady.

My reaction had been to ignore him and grab Molly by the arm, haul her none too gently from her chair and lead her outside without saying another word.

Me caveman, you Jane.

Beyond stupid.

Interestingly, however, Molly hadn't seemed to read too much into my actions. Maybe she thought I went around doing stuff like that on a regular basis.

Or maybe she wasn't used to men doing what I had, just as I wasn't used to doing what I had.

I gave her another long once-over and stifled a groan. The way she looked, I was surprised she didn't encounter reactions like mine at least daily.

She glanced at me. "That's fine, but it didn't really answer my question."

"No, I guess it didn't." I put my hat on to avoid completely crushing it in my hand. At times like this, the old-fashioned fedora served a double purpose. It helped me feel more professional. And I hoped that by extension it made me appear that way. It was my camouflage. My cue to switch gears and focus on something within my control when matters were veering beyond it.

I became all too aware of the wrinkles creasing my overcoat and the condition of the clothes underneath, wondering who I was kidding. I probably looked like Columbo on a bad day. And while Columbo had always gotten his man, women were few and far between.

I concentrated on the promenade before me, trying to ignore the *click-click* of her heels against the brick walkway. Unfortunately I had the feeling I'd be hearing it long after the sound had stopped.

I said, "We're going to a place on Bourbon. I need to ask the bartender a few questions."

"Regarding the Quarter Killer?"

"God, I hope not."

I didn't realize I'd said the words aloud until she stopped and stood staring at me.

I resisted the urge to smooth a tie that would

probably never be straight again. "My youngest sister has, well, fallen out of contact, and I'm trying to find her before my other two sisters bug me to death."

I wasn't clear on why I'd shared that. My personal life had no connection whatsoever to this woman, who had an agenda regarding her own sister.

"Do you think she's okay?"

I started walking again. "I'm sure she is. It's not the first time she's done something like this."

The *click-click* started again.

"But you're worried anyway."

Yes, it dawned on me, I *was* worried. "A man can't be a homicide detective and not be concerned when the twenty-one-year-old baby of the family won't answer her cell phone."

"Is there anything I can do?"

I squinted at her as we walked, my attention focused on her face rather than her too-hot body for the first time since spotting her in the bar. "No. But thanks. This is a family matter."

I caught her wince and cursed myself under my breath.

Here I was going on about family matters when she had her own very serious family matters to concern herself with.

I knew about her mother. Had been the one to contact her about Claire's death. Not only had Mona Laraway—now Sanchez—not seemed surprised, she hadn't seemed saddened by her daughter's death, either. When I tried to give her the information on how she could recover the body for burial, she'd just about hung up on me.

And five minutes later had been the first time I'd heard from Molly.

"So...what else have you been up to?" I asked. "Besides finding out there's been another murder?"

"I stopped by the prosecutor's office this morning."

Likely Bill Grissom had stonewalled her with his very efficient secretary.

"He seems nice but wasn't able to give me any more information than I already had."

"You met with him?"

She must have picked up on my surprise, because she smiled. "I have a few strings at my disposal."

She had more than a few, in my opinion. But right now I wasn't a good judge. I was more focused on the tightness of my groin than on anything going on in my brain.

"Well, that's not entirely true," she said, gesturing with her hand. "Not about the strings. Those are real enough. I mean about my not finding out anything I hadn't already known."

I didn't respond. Her comment was leading. Probably purposely so. And it had been a long time since leading comments had worked on me.

I felt her stare on my profile. "You didn't say anything about evidence pointing in another direction."

"Away from Lafitte," I said.

"Yes."

"Because there was really nothing to say."

"I figured that's what you'd say. That's why I called Akela Brooks. She met with me this morning."

It seemed Molly Laraway had been very busy today.

The mention of the FBI agent aggravated me. It wasn't that she'd been right about Claude Lafitte's innocence so much as her method for proving her point. Okay, so I'd been distracted and in no frame of mind to consider what she'd had to say with an open mind. But given her personal involvement with the suspect, I'd had good reason to shelve her arguments, as well.

"And?" I did a bit of obvious leading of my own.

"And she said the same thing Grissom did—there was evidence leading in a different direction, but she wouldn't tell me what the evidence was or in what direction it was leading."

Smart woman, Agent Brooks.

But her playing her cards close to her chest told me she was still working the case, something I'd already suspected given her presence at my questioning of Lafitte this morning. Molly's information had just verified my suspicions.

As far as I was concerned, that meant two too many damn cooks in the kitchen. A definite recipe for disaster.

We'd walked a few blocks down Bourbon Street from Canal, and I stopped in front of the open doorway to Club Bijou, a popular hangout for the Goth crowd and a place Zoe had been known to frequent. Just last month I'd met her there for a drink at her request.

"This it?" Molly asked.

"This is it." I took a deep breath. "Brace yourself."

MOLLY WASN'T TOO SURE why she would need to brace herself. And since she had no idea what she should brace herself against, she was wholly unprepared for the scene that greeted her just inside the open doorway to the club.

The walls were painted black and purple. And so were the people inside. A lot of people. And she got the impression that, Halloween week or not, the patrons would be dressed exactly the way they were now, minus a skull ring or two.

She tried to narrow her eyes from their wide-open position, watching as two women in their early twenties passed, their hair black with purple spiky streaks, their faces white and their lips painted black. She shuddered.

"Regular freak show," Alan said under his breath, although she couldn't be sure if he was talking to her or himself.

The place was crowded with people who looked almost exactly the same. There was something unsettling about her and Alan looking strange dressed the way they were when everyone in the place was dressed strangely. Clothes ranged from the very risqué with pushed-up cleavage and fishnet stockings to Elvira, Mistress of the Dark to Death himself.

Alan found a free stool at the end of the bar, closest to the door, and indicated for her to sit on it. With a few awkward tugs on her skirt and some careful maneuvering of her heels on the lower rung of the stool, she finally managed to do as he'd invited. He stood next to her.

"Halloween is a national holiday for this bunch," he mumbled.

The slow bass beat coming over the speakers placed along the walls filled the place with an ear-splitting rock song. Where in other places there might be a whoop of excitement and a race for the stage to dance, instead people moved toward the area in the back of the bar as if in a trance. Then they stopped and began moving in a jerky way. It took Molly a second to realize they were dancing.

Wow.

She leaned closer to Alan. "Does your sister dress like this?"

"Zoe?" he asked from where he was motioning toward the bartender. "No. She has a few piercings, and I've seen her with temporary color in her hair, but…" He shrugged and looked around. "Then again, who's to say? If she did dress this way, she could be in here and I wouldn't even know it."

The bartender had what looked like a silver dog

chain fastened from his brow to his nose, then down to a nipple revealed by an open leather vest. Molly couldn't help gaping. Didn't that hurt? It looked painful to her.

"Give us a couple of glasses of bourbon," Alan said. "And I was wondering…"

The bartender looked at Molly, then walked back down the bar, ignoring the beginning of Alan's question.

She listened to him curse.

"I'll be right back."

Molly opened her mouth to object, but he had already stepped from her side and was making his way through black and white and purple bodies down the bar.

Frankly she thought he should have waited until the bartender returned with their drinks to talk to him. And the bourbon arrived just as Alan made his way to the other end of the bar.

Molly smiled at the bartender and offered him the money for the drinks plus a hefty tip. He smiled back in a way that told her the money wasn't his only incentive.

She blinked at him, unable to decide if she liked the attention or if she should pack the dress she was wearing away forever when she got back to her hotel room tonight.

Finally he turned from her and made his way back down to the other end of the bar. Molly lifted one of the drinks, then downed it, the unfamiliar liquid burning a fiery trail down her throat. She coughed, then smiled at the girl next to her, who gave her a long look and sipped from her own martini glass, which held something iridescent red.

Molly stretched her neck and turned her attention back to Alan, who had finally gotten the chained bartender's attention. He held out something, and she saw the young man look at it, then shake his head. Alan's mouth was open, apparently midsentence, when the bartender walked away to wait on another customer.

"No luck?" she asked when Alan finally rejoined her.

His answer was another curse.

She nodded. "That's what I thought. Can I see the picture?"

He hesitated for a moment, looking at her. Then he held out the photo.

The four-by-six-inch shot had been folded back to focus on a pretty blonde with a smile as wide as Louisiana was long.

"She's lovely," she said.

She opened the picture so that the whole shot was revealed. Three beautiful young women were grouped together with Alan posed behind them, his wide arms more than long enough to envelop them all in a bearlike hug. She squinted and held the picture closer to the candle on the bar in front of her. At least, she thought it was Alan. The guy in the picture was different somehow from the man with her now, pretending not to care that she was studying the photo so closely. He was clean-shaven, had neatly trimmed hair and was minus his forever-present overcoat. And he was grinning with pride and happiness.

Definitely not the man she had come to know over the past couple of days.

He held out his hand for the picture.

Molly didn't give it back to him as she slid from the stool. "I'll be back in a minute."

# 9

THE RED OF MOLLY'S dress and the shine of her silky blond hair standing out in the sea of black was like a surreal movie shot as she made her way through the place, following the path I had taken a few minutes earlier. I couldn't seem to take my eyes from her. And neither, it appeared, could a lot of other guys in the place. Including the bartender.

I raised my eyebrows and watched as she motioned for him, and he went to her immediately.

The guy on the other side of me leaned closer. "Hot," he said.

I wondered what damage tugging on the ring in his nose would do. "Stick to your own kind."

He shrugged. "Hey, just because you like your meat well-done doesn't mean you don't want something fresh and raw every now and again."

I winced at the description of Molly and looked down at the two glasses in front of me. One was empty.

Molly laughed at something the bartender said, leaning across the bar so that her full breasts nearly spilled out of the top of her dress. I suddenly found it difficult to swallow. But somehow I managed as the bartender leaned closer to her, blocking my view.

I downed the other bourbon, then ran the back of the same hand across my mouth.

"Rafe's popular with the ladies," my new friend imparted. "I wouldn't leave her with him too long."

I took in the skinny guy; his ribs sticking out under his vest; his thin, tattooed arms; his quasi-Mohawk haircut. If that was the kind of guy Molly went for, the bartender could have her.

I looked down at myself. What was I talking about? I was reasonably sure she was attracted to me—and I was the type of guy not even I would date if I had been so inclined.

Molly was showing Rafe the picture of my sisters and me.

"You a cop?" the woman on the other side of me asked.

"What do you think?"

"I think you are." She swung toward me, revealing a jagged hole in her fishnet stockings that I wasn't altogether sure was an accident. Especially given the large silver safety pins holding the middle of the snag together. "I lost my handcuffs. How much to buy yours?"

I stared at her.

"Got it," Molly said, appearing at my side.

She got back up onto the stool, muddling my concentration. "Got what?"

"The name of the guy your sister's seeing."

I wasn't sure, but I think I growled at her. Just imagining my baby sister with someone like the kook behind the bar made my skin crawl.

"Let's get out of here," I said, grasping her upper arm.

The feel of her soft, fragrant skin under my fingers gave me pause. She smelled of gardenias.

She shrugged off my touch, but not before I caught a subtle shiver.

"We left the last place so quickly I didn't get a chance to enjoy my drink." She waved her empty glass at Rafe. "Another, please," she said when he came right over.

"Immediately."

I picked up my empty glass an instant too late and was forced to watch as Molly accepted a fresh drink while I went without.

"On the house," the bartender said.

I was feeling out of my element. And I didn't much like that.

Molly turned back to me. "Her boyfriend's name is Matthew Paulson. And neither of them has been around for about four or five days. Do you know anything about him?"

I grimaced. "I didn't even know Zoe was seeing anyone."

"Oh, and they don't call her Zoe here. She goes by the name Fawn."

"Fawn?" As in deer? Why would she have another name?

"From what I understand, everyone in the place has another name they go by. Matthew is called Paulie."

"My name's Thor," my new friend on the other side of Molly said.

I stared at him while Molly thrust her hand out. "Hi, Thor. I'm Molly and this is Alan."

Now she was getting friendly with the natives.

"You don't look like a Molly to me." The kid scrunched up his face. "If I had to give you a name, I'd say Siren."

"Why Siren?"

"You know, from Greek mythology." The guy grinned, revealing a mouthful of great teeth his parents had probably paid a fortune for. "Because you're enough woman to bring down any man."

"Jesus," I said under my breath. "Can we get out of here now?"

Molly ignored me. "What about him?" she asked Thor, waving her thumb in my direction.

The girl on my other side perked up. "Rourke," she said. "You know, after that actor who used to be a boxer and who's an actor again."

I glared at the girl.

Molly laughed.

"Not as he is now," she said. "Back in the beginning of his career, you know, when he was a real hottie. 'Cause he's a lot older than you now. I mean, you're kinda old but not that old, right?"

I wondered if I could arrest her on suspicion of criminal stupidity.

I was saved from a response by the vibrating of my cell phone. I fished it out of my inside coat pocket and looked at the display. *Home,* it read.

I stepped away from Molly and answered.

"Alan? Is that you? God, I can barely hear you."

Emilie.

"Hold on a sec."

I told Molly I was going outside, then stepped out onto the curb. That move alone slashed the volume of the music in half.

"Yeah?" I said, putting the phone back to my ear.

"I just wanted to find out if you've turned up anything yet."

I looked back inside the bar, where Molly was conversing with the girl who'd tried to buy my handcuffs. "Yeah. I got a line on her boyfriend."

"Good."

"You don't sound surprised she's seeing someone."

"She's been seeing someone for a month or so."

"Why didn't you say anything?"

"Because she wouldn't tell me what his name was or anything about him, that's why. I figured it would be best for you to find out on your own."

I rubbed my forehead, wondering what else my

sisters were leaving out. And what else lay in store for me. "Yeah, thanks."

When I closed the phone a few moments later, I turned to find Molly standing outside the club, leaning against the front of the building. Her arms were crossed under her breasts, her legs were crossed at the ankles, and she was looking at me like…

Hell, I don't know. Like she'd seen something about me that had surprised her. Something she apparently liked, if her smile was anything to go by.

"Everything okay?" she asked.

I was uncomfortable with her attention, so I began walking. She walked with me. "Emilie knew Zoe was seeing someone, but she didn't know who."

"And Emilie is…?"

"The oldest. Zoe's the youngest. And Laure is the middle sister."

She nodded, and I allowed her to set a leisurely stride down the promenade. Around us costumed people moved, bars thumped with both jazz and contemporary music, laughter rang. But somehow it felt as if none of it existed. I could still hear the *click-click* of her heels as if we were walking alone. I could smell her sweet scent as clearly as if I had my nose pressed against the curve of her neck.

I wanted her so badly I ached with it.

Stuffing my hands deep into the pockets of my overcoat, I concentrated on the walkway ahead of us.

"So," she said quietly. "Where to next?"

I jumped when I felt her hand slide around my arm, casually tucking itself between my elbow and waist.

She laughed quietly. "You're wound up."

She had no idea.

I slowed my steps, then stopped altogether. She moved so that she was in front of me, looking at me as if waiting to hear what I had to say.

And what did I have to say?

Her blue eyes were soft and open. Her pink lips all too kissable. She was unlike anything I'd ever seen before and hadn't known I wanted to see. She wasn't the naughty type of girl you took home for a one-night stand. She was the proper type you took home to mother. Yet I wanted to do things to her that had nothing to with proper and everything to do with soft moans and bare skin.

"Wait," she said quietly, shifting her weight from one of her sexily clad feet to the other. "Before you send me back to my hotel, I just want to do one thing."

I waited. "What?"

"This." And then she was kissing me.

BOURBON AND A HEAT SO hot it nearly seared her flesh. That's what Molly tasted the instant she pressed her lips against Alan's.

She wasn't entirely certain why she'd done what she had. All she knew was that right now, right at this moment, she felt like more of a woman than she'd felt in a very long time. Certainly since well before the death of her sister, when all color seemed to have been leached from her life.

And the man responsible for making her feel that way was this one standing in the middle of the sidewalk, kissing her.

Yes, she realized, melting against him like a sigh. He was kissing her.

It wasn't so much anything he'd said. From the moment their eyes had met at the Gas Lantern and he'd reacted possessively when she'd been asked to dance to the instant she'd seen the want in his eyes when he'd turned to find her waiting for him just now, his actions had spoke to her more intimately than any words. And she was so tuned in to them that she'd wanted her own actions to do the same…so she'd kissed him.

At first she'd been afraid he might push her away. She got the impression that despite how he might feel, he was determined to keep her at arm's length. Perhaps because of their roles, his as lead detective on her sister's case, hers as the twin sister of a murder victim. But as the hands on the clock budged around the dial, she was coming to understand that there was something more to his desire to keep her away. Something deeper and darker that drew her into its shadows.

Molly's hands moved to his chest, then down between the flaps of his trench coat. She slid her fingers inside, then around his waist, feeling heat warm her every cell even though she hadn't been cold. Despite his rumpled appearance, she felt rock-hard muscle beneath the cotton and was helpless to stop herself from tugging his shirt from the back of his slacks and pressing her fingertips to his taut skin. She heard his breath catch at the same time as he deepened their kiss.

She was distantly aware that he was moving them from the middle of the sidewalk, but didn't understand where until she felt the solid wall of a building against her back. The moment she leaned against it, he pressed his hard length against her and she gasped, grabbing hold of him tightly. She couldn't seem to get enough of him. His tongue against hers. His lips. The rasp of his stubble against her skin. His hands moving from her waist down over her hips, then back again, as if eager for a more intimate exploration but somehow holding himself in check, knowing where they were and what was appropriate. Although in this decadent city she got the impression that not a whole lot was inappropriate.

She snuggled inside his coat again, reveling in the feel of him so close. She ran her hands restlessly up and down his back—then froze when her fingers hit a hardness she hadn't anticipated. The metal of his gun in its holster around his left shoulder.

He must have picked up on her hesitation because he reluctantly removed his mouth and leaned his forehead against hers.

"This is crazy," he said, grinding out the words as if battling unseen demons.

She nodded and removed her hands. For one sweet moment she'd allowed herself to forget who he was, who she was, and for the first time since she'd learned of Claire's death had allowed herself the luxury of forgetting that her sister was gone.

He shifted to move away, but for a reason she couldn't fathom, she held tight.

"Please. Not yet," she murmured, closing her eyes, not caring if she looked desperate or clingy. "It's been a very long time since I've felt this kind of connection to another person."

# 10

THERE WERE A FEW THINGS a living, breathing male wasn't equipped to resist. And at the top of the list was a beautiful woman who smelled like sin and who wanted to be touched.

I swallowed thickly and slid my hands from Molly's lush hips to wrap them around her waist. She felt so good, tucked against my body just so, that I didn't want the moment to end, either. My throbbing erection rested against her trembling stomach, making me want far more, but I restrained myself. Something I wasn't used to doing. It had been a long, long time since I hadn't taken the next natural step and suggested that the two of us retire to my apartment. And while I wasn't entirely sure why I was resisting now, I knew in my gut that it was the right thing to do. No matter how enticing her breasts felt pressed against my chest. Or how damn inviting she smelled and felt.

I knew that if I wanted, I could have her. Walk her back to her hotel nearby and seduce my way into her bed and between her soft thighs. But some invisible force held me back. Her reaction a moment ago, when she'd accidentally made contact with my police-issue firearm, had shuddered through me as surely as if I was the one who'd had a cold bucket of reality dumped over my head.

I felt her hands move from where they were plastered against my back. Her fingertips worked their way under the hem of my shirt and touched my bare skin. I hissed a breath.

"Decide, Molly. Because in two seconds I'm afraid that decision will be taken from us."

Her fingers stilled and her head shifted from where her cheek rubbed against mine. She looked deep into my eyes.

"I want you," she whispered. "But I'm not sure if I should have you. I… You… I don't know. Everything's so confused right now."

*Tell me about it.*

But crystal clear was the fact that she was right—sleeping together probably wasn't the smartest thing to do right now. I still had the unfortunate situation with Captain Hodge's wife hovering over my head like a guillotine waiting to sever me from a career I'd spent more than ten years building. To sleep with the sister of a murder victim—especially such a high-profile victim of the Quarter Killer—would be inviting even more trouble.

Molly licked her lips slowly and I groaned.

Screw trouble.

I bent my head and kissed her again.

THE FOLLOWING MORNING Molly woke with a start, alone in her bed, her skin covered in sweat.

She reached out to crowd the free pillow close to her chest, wishing that she—that both she and Alan—had given themselves over to the molten desire that had filled them both the night before. But just when it had looked as if he might follow her inside her room after walking her back to the hotel, he had kissed her a final time and said good-night instead.

She closed her eyes and attempted to calm the erratic beating of her heart, her mind going to the dream that had awakened her. Rather, the nightmare. Her unsettled subconscious mind had taken up where she and Alan had left off, and they'd made love all over her hotel room, no place safe from their need for each other.

Then she'd been lying naked, with her head lolling over the foot of the bed, as Alan had slid into her to the hilt. At the same time as she'd climaxed, a big dark cloud had appeared where Alan's face had been and she'd felt a cold knife slice through the flesh of her neck.

Molly lifted a hand to the area in question as another image came to mind. A memory this time. She and Claire had been fourteen, full of teenage angst, lying across the double bed they'd shared in a rented trailer near the Michigan border. One side of the double bed had been flush against the paneled wall, and she'd been the one to sleep there, using the wall to prop up whatever book she was reading.

*Have you ever thought about death?* Claire had asked, lying in the opposite direction so that her feet were next to Molly's head. Her sister had been leafing through a teen fanzine while Molly had been reading a tattered copy of *Wuthering Heights* she'd checked out of the school library.

Claire had sighed and performed the wiggling act required to roll over in the narrow space. *I mean, beyond wanting to poison the latest jerk Mom brings home.*

That was why they'd been in their room. Because their mother had come home from a nearby bar with another guy whose name no one would remember next week.

*I guess so,* Molly had answered, her attention stolen from Heathcliff's musings. *Why?*

*I don't know. I mean, ever since Grandma died and all, I've been wondering what it's like. And thinking about all the ways it can happen.* She'd shuddered. *I think being strangled would be the worst.*

*That's murder,* Molly had pointed out.

*Yes, but you still die.*

Molly had considered what she'd said and stared at the ceiling, where her sister had taped pictures of Madonna and the Backstreet Boys. *I think drowning would be the worst way to go.*

Claire had lifted up onto her elbows and stared at her. *Oh, my God. You're right. That would be the absolute worst. I mean, when you're underwater, time must seem to drag on forever.*

Molly wasn't sure what made her remember that day so long ago. The topic of death, perhaps. And the fact that for some godforsaken reason her sister had been obsessed with the subject matter. Not just on the day she'd remembered; rather it seemed to have been an ongoing obsession with Claire, similar conversations periodically taking place over the years.

Until death had finally claimed her.

Molly shivered and forced herself out of bed although it was barely dawn. After showering and getting dressed, she pulled the box containing Claire's things on top of the bed again and methodically took the items out and laid them down one by one. She'd honored the same routine since arriving in the city and claiming the belongings. She kept hoping that something would pop out at her, something that would help her finally lay Claire to rest.

IF I'D BEEN IN BAD shape yesterday morning, I was in even worse shape today. I told myself it was because of the bottle of bourbon I'd turned to after turning Molly away. But the truth was that the damn woman remained with me even after I'd left her at her hotel room. She was there when I closed my eyes and when I opened them. I knew a sense of longing so pronounced that it was almost difficult to keep putting one foot in front of the other.

But forging ahead, concentrating on the job rather than the woman, was exactly what I had to do.

Pounding the pavement, checking with snitches and going over and over the same ground again was part of the job. A part I sometimes hated. Then again, if a case was easy to solve, it usually meant that not everything was as it appeared. Along the lines of "If it looks too good to be true, it probably is." Case in point: my arrest of Claude Lafitte for the murder of Molly's sister. He'd been at the scene of the crime, had taken FBI agent Akela Brooks hostage and had run with her when NOPD officers had tried to take him into custody.

Everything had been so neat, so tidy—and it had been so far off base that the already shaky foundation of my career had begun to crumble around the edges.

After a morning of dead ends I slapped another file down on top of my desk in the middle of Robbery/Homicide division's bullpen, then reached out to keep the pile from toppling off as I sat down. My head felt a heartbeat away from exploding, and my throat was raw.

"You don't look so good."

I stared at John Roche, a junior detective who had turned from everybody's buddy to my own personal tormentor as of late.

"I mean, you look even worse today than you usually do. Which is saying a lot. What, did you sleep in a garbage can last night?"

"Bite me, Roche."

The other man chuckled. "You've got a visitor waiting downstairs."

Shit. It looked like I was never going to get a chance to tackle the mess on my desk. A mess I was beginning to think might hold the answers if only because time and circumstances weren't allowing me to go through it.

"Who is it?"

"I don't know, but two of the desk sergeants have already tried to pick her up, so I'd get down there before someone else makes off with her."

Molly. It had to be. She was the only one I could think of who might stop by the precinct to see me. Maybe she had come up with something.

Then again, the way my luck was running lately, I'd go down there to find Astrid waiting for me.

No. Even John would know who she was. And Astrid wouldn't dare be so blatant.

Would she?

"Oh, and Alan?" John said. "The captain wants to see you."

I stood staring at him. "Why didn't you say that first?"

"Because it was more fun telling you this way."

I grabbed my hat from the rack where I'd hung it and made my way to Captain Seymour Hodge's office. While we might work in the same office, thankfully I didn't cross paths with him often. Mostly by design. I knew the times he was in and went out of my way not to be there when he was.

Call me stupid, but I didn't much like being around a guy who had my balls in a vise.

His secretary motioned at me to go in, and I knocked briefly on the door before stepping inside Hodge's office.

"You wanted to see me?"

He was standing at the window, looking out at the street beyond. He turned to stare at me. "You look like hell, Detective."

I rubbed my chin. "Did you call me in here to discuss my personal hygiene? Because if you did, I'll promise to shave tomorrow and make a run to the cleaners and we can be done with this meeting."

The bad blood between Hodge and me went way back to when he was a senior homicide detective and I was new to the job. We'd rubbed each other the wrong way from the word *go.* He was always the well-dressed dandy, while I was always Johnny-on-the-spot, ferreting out clues while Hodge played politics with the higher-ups. I hadn't known at the time it was because he'd had his eye on the captain's office.

So basically the animosity between us went well beyond the fact that I'd slept with Hodge's wife. Sure, they'd been estranged at the time, but that didn't matter now that they'd reconciled.

Or was that it? Did Hodge know his wife was

calling me on the sly? That I'd stopped by to see her, no matter how brief or innocent the visit?

Damn.

Hodge stood to his full height, hands behind his back. "Two dead bodies, no suspects. Where do we stand in the Quarter Killer case, Chevalier?"

We. Now there was a word for you. *We* didn't stand anywhere when it came to the case. Rather *I* was standing at the edge of a very tall cliff and knew Hodge was waiting for an excuse to shove me right off it.

"I have no new information to offer," I said, participating in the stare-off he apparently wanted when I knew I should probably look away.

"Find it. Now."

I felt my back teeth grinding together, increasing the intensity of my headache. "Is there anything else…sir?"

His eyes narrowed. "I don't think I have to remind you of all that is on the line here, Detective."

"No, you don't."

"Very well, then. That's it."

I turned and walked from the room. I didn't much like the little reminder that I was being watched.

At any rate, I had a woman waiting in the lobby for me. And if I was going to go down, it might as well be because of a woman.

Interestingly it was neither Molly nor Astrid chatting with probably the only sergeant who hadn't tried to pick her up, only because Pierre was gay.

"Valerie," I said, greeting my ex-wife.

She kissed both my cheeks, then stood back to take me in. "Jesus, Al, you look like you woke up on the wrong side of a vodka bottle."

"Bourbon," I said, ignoring that it was the third time in so many minutes somebody had commented on my appearance. Maybe I should start taking a look in the bathroom mirror with the light on.

"Oh. And you don't smell all that hot, either."

"What do you want, Val?"

"I came by to take you to lunch."

I looked down at my watch, convinced it couldn't already be noon. But there it was. A quarter after.

I dry-washed my face.

"I'm half tempted to make you go home to shower first, though."

"Hey, Chevalier, why don't you introduce us to the lady?" a sergeant across the room called out.

While it seemed like only a month had passed since Valerie had finally dumped me, five years had gone by. Years that had been kind to her. If it was possible, she looked even better now than she had then. Her shiny dark hair was cut to a flattering shoulder length that accentuated its silky texture. Her tan slacks and black clingy top revealed a body in better shape than it had ever been.

As I had countless times, I asked myself why it was I couldn't have fallen in love with the woman that was everything any man could want.

Still, things weren't all bad. I'd exchanged a wife for a best friend. A guy could do worse.

"Come on," she said, linking her arm in mine. "I only have an hour. And the boss is being a bitch this morning."

"I thought your boss was a guy."

"Your point being?" She smiled wide.

"You can't call a man a bitch."

"Sure I can. Just like I can call a woman a wuss. What, are you going to arrest me for abuse of a gender-specific noun?"

Val always had a way of making me smile.

"What's on your mind?" I asked as we walked to a nearby restaurant that lay between the precinct and her office, where she worked as a title agent. "Have you found out something about Zoe?"

"Actually, this isn't about your sisters. Well, not in the way you think, anyway."

I put my hat on and grumbled, "I hate when you talk in circles."

"Let me make it easy for you then. Emilie and Laure are worried about you."

I stopped in the middle of the sidewalk, causing her to stop, as well.

She heaved a heavy sigh. "Look, Alan, I know you don't like anyone interfering with your family. And I'll be the first to admit that I don't have a clue what goes on in your day-to-day life—hell, I didn't even know when we were married. I do know that whatever's going on, it's visibly affecting you." She plucked at the lapel of my rumpled overcoat.

"Is this another crack about my appearance?"

She looked at me long and hard, and I read the concern in her brown eyes. "No. It's not."

The somberness of her words, combined with the lack of an attempt at a joke, told me how serious she was.

"Alan, I remember how you were when we first met."

Uh-oh. It was never good when a woman brought up something from your past together. It usually meant I was about to get slapped across the face with it.

"I know I never said anything, and you were pretty good at keeping it from the girls, drinking only after they'd gone to bed. But I remember many a night spent listening to you after you'd locked yourself in the library. The sound of bourbon being poured into a glass and of an increasingly empty bottle hitting the desk next to it."

I blinked at her, having forgotten about that time. Maybe it was because I'd thought it was okay. After all, that's what I'd grown up watching my father do, whether it was alone or with visiting friends gathered in his library to smoke cigars.

"I was worried about you then, but I never said anything. I figured that was how you dealt with everything that had been forced onto you." She looked down at her feet, then up at a couple pushing a baby stroller across the street. "Anyway, those nights became more and more frequent…."

I blinked at her, unable or incapable of believing what she was saying to me.

If there was one thing we'd always shared, it was trust. I trusted Valerie with my life. I trusted her opinion. More than that, I cared what she thought about me, damn it. Not unlike the way I felt about my sisters.

"You need help, Alan. Professional help." She shook her head. "I'm sorry. I didn't mean to just dump it all on you like that." She smiled. "Come on. Maybe we'll both feel better after we've put a little something in our stomachs."

# 11

MOLLY SAT IN THE GAS LANTERN on a stool at the end of the bar, wearing something much more conservative than the sexy dress she'd had on the night before. Still, a lone woman in a bar seemed to attract a lot of attention no matter what she wore. The guy who had asked her to dance last night had asked her again tonight. She'd said no. And it had taken the owner, Jack Cadieux, to fend off the guy.

Molly looked at her watch again. He was over a half hour late. And while she had his number at the precinct, she didn't think it a good idea to call there since their association was supposed to be on the hush-hush.

She nudged her watch around her wrist and wet her lips with the splash of bourbon she'd ordered and was still nursing, then took out a few bills from her purse for a tip.

"Any message?" Jack asked her as he dried a clean glass. He remembered her and knew she was waiting for Alan.

She shook her head. "No, thanks."

"Don't mention it."

Molly walked from the bar feeling more exposed tonight than she had in the skimpy dress. Of course, last night she'd been with Alan, and he'd seemed more than capable of taking care of her with or without his badge.

Tonight…

She shivered as the wind pushed an empty soda can down the street and a group of people on the corner laughed, the sound carrying on the night air. Tonight she felt as though ghosts hovered everywhere. Especially that of her sister.

Heading in the direction of her hotel, she tried to keep her steps normal and unhurried even though her heart beat thickly in her chest, urging her to pick up the pace. After all, there was a killer on the loose. Two killers, if Alan was right and the murders at the hotel weren't connected.

"Hey, lady, got a dollar?" a man standing alone on the corner asked.

She shook her head and hastened her step. A taxi turned the corner in front of her, and she raised her hand to hail it, never more relieved than when it stopped.

She started to give him the address for the hotel, then changed her mind and gave him the address to Alan's place. If he wasn't there, she could always continue on to the hotel. If he was…

She shivered again, but this time for an entirely different reason.

Throughout the day, memories of last night had intruded, making her lips tingle and her body throb. If their parting had been a ploy to cool her desire, it wasn't working. If anything, she wanted him even more. She felt a pulse-quickening awareness that followed her everywhere she went, regardless of whether she was consciously thinking of him.

She slid off her right loafer and rubbed the arch of her foot. She wasn't sure if it was because of the heels she'd worn last night or the flat shoes she'd traded them for today, but her feet hurt like the devil. Which made it just as well that she'd hailed the cab. She'd done more walking in the past few days than she had in the past few years.

"This it, lady?"

She realized that the taxi had pulled up outside Alan's place. She spotted his car parked on the opposite curb. "Yeah, this is it."

She paid the driver, then climbed out and stood in the middle of the street as he pulled away. She took out her pad and quickly found the page noting the apartment number of Alan's place. 3B. She looked up at the dark windows, watching as a light went on, then another, and knew a moment of hesitation. What if he wasn't alone?

She cleared her throat. Well, if he wasn't alone, then it was just as well that she found out now. Besides, she had no claim on him. They had kissed. So what?

In truth, she hoped that he wasn't with someone and that he had thought about her today as much as she'd thought about him.

At any rate, there was only one way to find out.

THE FIRST THING I DID after letting myself into my apartment was switch on all the lights. Then I stood blinking at the place to regain my bearings.

The past few hours since lunch with Val had been hell on earth. Forensics chief Steven Chan had verified what I suspected—namely that the two murders were very likely unconnected. Two different murder weapons had been used. And while that in and of itself wasn't enough to build a case on, when combined with the other circumstantial evidence, it was. Which meant I had two killers running around loose now instead of one.

Of course, while I tried to blame my distraction strictly on the investigation, my mind kept straying to the conversation I'd had with Val over gumbo.

*You've got to regain control over your life, Alan.*

Her words echoed through my mind as I shucked my overcoat, then everything else I had on, dropping the items in my wake as I headed for the bathroom and the shower beyond. I purposely avoided looking into the mirror if only because I was afraid of what I'd see.

Damn, damn, damn. As I stood under the punishingly hot spray and quickly scrubbed myself down, I thought about what Val had said about the girls. My sisters. No longer girls but adults. Adults who were worried about me but incapable of approaching me themselves because...well, because I was like a parent to them, and kids didn't broach such topics with their parents.

I tried to focus on the case, on the evidence Steven had picked up from Frederique Arkart's body, but all I could seem to focus on was the fact that it was late and I had yet to have a drink. My body ached with the need for it. My throat yearned for the taste of it.

And I hated myself for both.

I leaned my hand against the shower stall, wondering whether the hot water would last if I just stood there until the craving passed. Only the wall, the mirror and I knew that it wouldn't pass. Val was right. Throughout my adult life I'd turned to liquor when things got tough. But this time...well, this time I'd gone too far. While my drinking hadn't crept into my daytime hours, all signs pointed to it going that route, if not today or tomorrow, then the day after that. And when that happened...

Truthfully this time of day was most difficult, when I returned to a place that wasn't so much home as a location to store my bourbon and pass out on the secondhand bed that had come with the apartment.

I ran my hand over my face, the self-loathing inside taking over.

*It's a vicious cycle,* Val had said, reaching for my

hand. I'd pulled it away. *You hate yourself for drinking and it's that same hate that makes you reach for the bottle to obliterate it.*

*What are you all of a sudden?* I'd said, agitated. *My AA sponsor?*

She'd ignored my snide remark and smiled. *If that's what it takes. Although I'm pretty sure a person has to have been where you're at in order to understand what you're going through.*

And, of course, Valerie had never been there. She'd always been completely in control of her life. Or thought she was. Except when it had come to her hope that our marriage would somehow work.

I closed my eyes and turned my face into the hard spray. Was that what she was doing again? Working on a lost cause that was so far gone it was beyond hope?

Hearing what sounded like a knock at the front door, I opened my eyes and listened. Another knock.

Christ. That was all I needed—a visitor now.

But seeing as I'd switched off my cell phone a couple of hours ago and that I had yet to check the three messages I'd seen blinking on my answering machine, the visitor could be just about anybody, including someone sent over from the precinct.

I turned off the water and grabbed a towel, hoping like hell that was who it was. Because if I found Astrid standing in the hall—or even Val—I didn't know what I was capable of just then.

I wrenched the door inward to find Molly instead.

"Oh," she said, apparently startled by the obviously irritated action.

It was then that I realized I'd missed our meeting at the Gas Lantern.

"Um, can I come in?"

I stood for a long moment gripping the door with one hand, the towel around my hips with the other.

"Why the hell not? Everyone in my life seems to be doing what they want anyway."

I released the door and strode back toward the bathroom, on my way snatching up the clothes I'd left littering the floor. I stepped into the bathroom, then closed the door, standing for long moments, not really sure of where I was and what I was doing.

Oh, I knew physically where I stood. I just wasn't sure where in the hell my head was at. By all rights, I should have told Molly now wasn't a good time, then slammed the door in her pretty face. *I* didn't want her to see me this way. Hell, I didn't want to see me this way.

I found I was staring at my reflection in the mirror. I blinked, taking in the dripping hair hanging over my brow, the water clinging to my torso and shoulders and the almost savage expression on my face.

Val was right. I was losing it.

MOLLY STOOD IN THE middle of the small, spartan apartment and wrapped her arms around herself, fighting both the desire to leave and the need to stay.

Alan had been more than rude. He'd been...well, rude about being rude. But there had been something almost pleading in his eyes. While he'd radiated sarcasm and tension, for a moment she'd viewed in his expression an emotion she could only liken to relief and...well, hope.

An emotion she felt whenever she was around him, even when he was brusque with her. No matter what their many differences, she felt they shared a sameness that went beyond their mutual goal to find her sister's killer. Two injured souls reaching out for one another, consequences and conscious thought be damned.

She looked around. Up until now she'd thought her day had been pretty crappy. Ending with being stood up by the man who was presently a little too quiet behind the bathroom door. But she suspected that whatever she'd faced had been nothing compared to what Alan was going through.

Without realizing she was doing so, she picked up his overcoat from the floor, hung it on a hook near the door along with his hat, then moved on into the kitchen. There were a few coffee mugs in the sink, along with a couple of plates, but nothing serious. After cleaning out the coffeemaker, she put a fresh pot on to boil, then found two clean mugs and placed them on the counter, which she leaned against while she watched the open doorway for signs of life from the other room.

In her first few years of college she'd lived in

plenty of places similar to this one. Furnished apartments that looked as if they hadn't been painted since the 1970s. They were in-between places she never put her stamp on but merely saw in the morning when she got up and in the evening right before she went to bed, the time in between spent on campus and at the library, where she had computer access and where she preferred to do her studying.

The coffeemaker stopped spitting, and she turned to pour the hot liquid into two mugs, not much caring about the late hour.

"What are you doing?"

At the harsh sound of Alan's voice from the doorway, Molly nearly dropped the mugs she'd just picked up. She turned. He'd gotten dressed into a pair of creased slacks and a wrinkled shirt that hung open to reveal the washboard abs she had felt last night but was now seeing.

"I, um, made coffee," she said, holding out a mug for him. "I hope you don't mind."

He merely stood considering her for long moments, then finally reached out to take what she offered.

She took a long, fortifying sip from her cup, wrinkling her nose at the bitter taste of his preferred blend. "Have you lived here long?"

He looked around as if just now seeing the place for the first time.

"I mean, no offense, but I've been here five minutes and I'm already feeling sorry for myself."

He appeared to find amusement in her comment. "Five years."

She nodded. "Long time."

"Too long."

He turned and walked into the other room, which was a combination living room/bedroom. To her right was a double bed, unmade. To her left, a threadbare sofa and chair positioned around a television that looked as old as the furniture.

She gestured toward the set. "That thing even have a remote?"

He reached out and picked something up from the chair arm, then tossed it to the coffee table.

"Let me guess," she said. "Child support and alimony."

His gaze narrowed on her face. Suddenly she felt the lightheartedness she was trying to affect melt away from her.

"Three younger sisters who are living in a family house that's paid for but that has upkeep bills that are more than they can manage."

She blinked. The three beautiful young women in the picture. "Why don't you sell it?"

He sat down in the chair. She slowly rounded the sofa and sat down.

"Because it's been in the family since it was built two hundred years ago."

Molly hadn't had a chance to play tourist and visit the Garden District, but she'd seen enough pictures in the books on New Orleans she'd bought to know he was likely referring to one of the older places.

"And alimony."

She blinked.

"Although Valerie hasn't cashed a check I've sent her in over three years."

Molly took another sip of her coffee, then placed the cup on the table. "How long were you married?"

"Five years."

"Children?"

He shook his head, then fell silent for long moments. Molly swallowed hard, listening to the sounds of his neighbors. Downstairs, a couple shouted at each other. Somewhere a cat meowed. And the scent of fried okra that had been strong in the hall was subtler here yet still present.

"Do your feet hurt?"

She blinked at Alan, only then realizing that she'd slid off her left shoe and was rubbing her arch.

She smiled. "Yeah. I guess I'm not used to doing the type of walking I've been doing here."

He put his coffee cup down and motioned for her to put her foot on his knee.

Molly's heart stopped outright in her chest.

She'd never had a man offer to rub her feet before. The offer was so foreign and so tempting that she didn't quite know how to respond.

But she was happy for the change in atmosphere and didn't want to go back to feeling unwelcome, so she hesitantly lifted her foot. He gently grasped it and rested it against his knee. The instant his thumb slid down her arch, serious tingles erupted throughout her body.

"I'm sorry about...well, being short with you when I opened the door."

Molly found it hard to push words through her suddenly tight throat. "That's okay. It's just that when you didn't show at the bar tonight, I..."

She what? She'd worried for his well-being?

No, she realized. That wasn't it at all. Rather she'd been looking for exactly what he was giving her now. And she didn't mean a foot massage, although his lazy, knowing moves were igniting all sorts of interesting sensations. Rather she'd needed to see the awareness in his eyes when he looked at her. As he was looking at her now....

# 12

THERE WAS SOMETHING relaxing about touching Molly. By concentrating on the rhythmic motions of my thumbs and fingers against her smooth, warm skin, I was somehow able to force aside the demons that had been torturing me the better part of the day and focus solely on her.

Of course, I could have done that even without the foot massage. Molly made it damn difficult to think about anything but her, whether she was in the room or not.

Truth was, she offered me something that was being denied me in every other area of my life right now. Something intangible but important. Something that grounded me in a strange way. Something that made me want her with an intensity that was more powerful than even the bourbon I still craved.

I idly wondered why she'd gone for the coffee. In plain view were at least four bourbon bottles in various stages of emptiness. Next to the bed, on top of the ancient television and on the kitchen table and counter.

Probably seeing so many bottles of the same make of liquor had sent her scrambling to make coffee for me, lest she discover I needed sobering up.

I grimaced. Definitely not a good first impression. Then again, I hadn't been looking to impress anybody. Hadn't been looking to impress anyone for a long time. Astrid…well, Astrid had been a hot, forbidden lay, our one liaison taking place at her house. The other women before and in between had been one-night stands that hadn't stuck around long enough to see what the apartment looked like in the light of day, mostly because I had shown them the door before they could even catch their breath.

Yet, despite the impression she may have gotten, here was Molly, looking like if I got up right now and carried her to the bed, she would go willingly.

And I wasn't moving.

What did that mean? Except that I was crazy?

More than likely it meant that I knew I didn't have the right even to think about touching someone as sweet and beautiful as Molly Laraway, no matter how smart she was or how adult and capable of making her own decisions.

"Mmm, that feels good." Her whisper reached my ears.

I cleared my throat. "So…what did you accomplish today?"

She'd relaxed against the sofa, looking like a

swath of pure silk poured over my unworthy couch. She considered me through the fringe of her lashes. "Uh-uh. You first."

I encircled the upper part of her right foot with both hands, pressing her toes with my thumb. "Some forensics results are in. The evidence proves we're dealing with two separate killers."

I caught her shiver, although I couldn't be sure if it was a result of my attentions or her reaction to the news.

"You?" I asked, trying to focus on something beyond what I was doing, because my attention was starting to wander. My gaze took in her slender ankles and a portion of her shapely calves where her tan slacks had fallen back. Her breasts were full and round under her clingy black top. I realized she was wearing something similar to what Val had had on earlier. But my reaction to the clothes—or, more importantly, the woman underneath—couldn't have been more different.

"I went to the scene of the crime."

I stared at her. "The Josephine?"

She nodded.

I thought of her inside the hotel that may have at different times been the talk of the town, either as an upscale place to stay or as a brothel, but was now not even a stop for prostitutes. "And?"

She smiled. "And it was closed."

My hands slowed. Since the day I'd responded to

the call reporting Molly's sister's murder, I'd never known Josie Villefranche to close the front doors. I was familiar with the place long before that, going back to her grandmother, and I couldn't remember a single solitary time when I'd seen the place closed.

"I was reading the sign in the window when a guy who said he worked there came up."

"Philippe Murrell."

"Yes. He seemed surprised by the sign and was more than a little upset."

So Josie had closed the hotel and hadn't told her staff. I frowned.

"Oh, please don't stop."

I realized I'd ceased my motions. I gazed into her blue eyes that were almost black with desire.

Damn. I hadn't meant for my actions to arouse her. Then again, who was I kidding? Touching her left me more than a little hot and bothered. Why should she be any different?

I released her foot and moved to stand. If I didn't do something soon, I'd end up taking her right on the couch.

Her reaction was quick and kept me from passing.

"Alan," she said quietly.

The scent of gardenias teased my nose, and her hair shone almost white in the bright light.

"Molly, I…getting sexually involved isn't a good idea right now."

She slowly lifted her hand, trailing a finger along

my bare chest between the open flaps of my shirt. A trail of fire burned its way straight to my groin.

"Oh, I think some parts of it would be good," she said, leaning in to kiss my neck. "Very, very good."

Christ.

She kissed her way up my jawline, both her hands on my chest now, making their way down, then around to my back inside my shirt. I hissed a deep breath as she pressed her soft body against me at the same time her mouth reached mine.

At the gentle touch of Molly Laraway I was a puddle of raging male hormones at her beautiful feet.

I entwined my hand in her hair, meaning to pull her away, but instead hauled her closer. So soft. So sweet. So damn sexy.

Her quickened breathing filled my ears. Or was that mine? Both, I think. My blood thickened as she pressed herself against me, apparently catching on to my condition, as she made a little sound in her throat and edged closer still. My erection hardened further, letting me know in no uncertain terms what it wanted. And that was to be inside Molly's slick, hot flesh—now.

Which was precisely the reason I tightened my hands in her hair—to keep them from wandering. The action also held her still. I took full advantage of the result and plundered her mouth, focusing all my need on the relative safety of her swollen lips, her seeking tongue.

Then I felt her fingertips at the front of my trousers. The danger zone.

While I could control my own actions to some degree, it appeared that, short of handcuffs, I couldn't control Molly's. And she seemed determined to push this as far as it could go, the hell with the consequences.

Within moments her hot fingers slid against the hard length of my erection. I dragged in a deep breath and pulled my mouth away slightly from hers, reveling in the feel of her touching me. Damn, but it felt good. Too good.

She popped the fastener on my slacks and tugged down the zipper until I felt air on me, then her fingers again. She encircled the engorged length, then brushed her thumb over the tip, effectively reminding me that I was but a man. And with her doing what she was, well, there was only so much I could take before my self-control snapped.

A millimeter away from that point, she released me, then grabbed the hem of her shirt, pulling it up and forcing me to remove my hands from her hair. She wore the skimpiest of white bras, practical yet sexy as hell against her pale skin. Her breasts were perfect globes begging for attention I was loath not to give them.

I fastened my mouth over a protruding nipple through the shiny material of her bra, pulling it in deep. She gasped, stretching her neck to give me easier access while I supported her back with my hands. Those same hands found the fastener, and I popped it open, causing the bra to slip down over her breasts. She moved to take it the rest of the way off, but I was too impatient for that, eager to taste her bare flesh against my tongue. And that's what I did, pulling her other nipple into my mouth and suckling deeply, reveling in the clean taste of her.

Damn, had a woman ever tasted so good to me? Had I ever experienced such a state of need for a woman while she still had her pants on? I smoothed my hands along the column of her back. So soft. So firm.

She apparently regained a portion of her bearings and pushed my own shirt back, giving her access to my shoulders. She ran her tongue across my collarbone, then over my right bicep before kissing my skin, driving me insane with the image of her paying such rapt attention to another area of my anatomy.

Giving up all pretense of control, I swept her up into my arms and carried her toward the bed. She clung to me easily, her eyes staring deeply into mine. I laid her across the tousled bedsheets, marveling at the needy expression on her face, the wildness of her hair. I'd moved well beyond questioning what she saw in me and acted on pure instinct instead, peeling away her bra, then reaching for the front of her slacks, all the while my gaze glued to her beautiful face. Within moments her slacks and panties lay with mine on the floor, and she was pushing my shirt the rest of the way off.

I reached to switch off the lamp.

She caught my hand. “No. Don’t. I don’t want this to happen in the shadows. I want it to happen in plain light, where we both know what’s happening.”

And what was happening?

As I pressed my palm against her stomach, sliding it down toward the triangle of soft fleece between her legs, I was afraid to answer that question, fearful of what I’d find lurking beneath the desire blinding me to nearly all else. I might honor her request for light, but the openness she demanded was a little more difficult in coming. Probably because it wasn’t one of my strong suits when it came to the opposite sex. I’d spent far too much time hiding my real self to step out into the light. To allow Molly to see me, all of me. My identity was built on shadows and darkness. To cast that aside now would be to deny who I was. To bare myself not only physically but emotionally… well, even if I’d wanted to do that, I don’t think I could have.

So I forced myself to focus on the physical instead.

MOLLY WATCHED MYRIAD emotions flicker across Alan’s face. His expression was almost savage. And while the light revealed a handsomeness not even she had glimpsed until now, the stubble marring his face clung like a shadow that refused to be chased away. She wondered if that was a fitting metaphor for the man himself.

His fingers slowly trailed from her stomach to her springy pubic hair, then touched her tight bud. Her eyes drifted closed and she swallowed hard, all thought blurring from her mind.

The instant she'd stood to face him, barring him from an avenue for escape, she'd known she'd made an important decision to force whatever was happening between them to its natural conclusion…or beginning. She couldn't say which it would be, only knew an intense desire to find out. There were too many unanswered questions swirling around in her life now. She needed to exercise a power over those she could. And with Alan leaning over her now, his body slender and muscular, his eyes full of need for her at the same time as his jaw clenched in what appeared to be a desperate effort to keep control, she knew she was traveling the right path.

He needed this as much as she did. She felt that with everything that she was. They both longed for a connection that transcended them and their bodies and rational thought.

She slowly opened her thighs to him, bending her knees to gain leverage as she lifted her vulva into his touch. She heard his groan and opened her eyes to watch him watching her. Then she reached for his obvious arousal, curving her fingers around the thick width. So long. So hard. She could virtually feel his heartbeat there, just beyond the silken, stiff flesh.

She wanted him to lose control. Needed to know she was the cause of it.

She gently squeezed and drew her hand down, then back up again, watching as he groaned and threw his head back. Such a simple touch. Such a feral response.

Then he was grasping her hips and turning her over.

Molly was caught off guard at first, her face pressed against a pillow that smelled of him. She moved to turn back around. She wanted to see him. Yearned to see his face during the progression of their lovemaking.

He held her still.

Then he was touching her again, stroking her slick heat from behind, and she was the one groaning. She heard a drawer open and close, then a condom packet being torn, and before she could catch her breath, he was stealing it away from her again by positioning his hardness against her softness.

He paused.

Molly lay still, anticipating the moment when he would breach her. When his flesh would meld with her flesh and they would topple over into the next level of sweet sensation.

She felt his fingertips on her back, caressing her. Down and up. Bumps peppered her skin at his gentle attention, her nipples pulsing against the sheets. His touch reached the top of her buttocks. Molly instinctively arched her back, lifting her hips to both give him easier access and tempt a more intimate touch.

Then he was grasping her hips and entering her, thrusting all coherent thought from her mind and setting her every cell on fire.

He filled her to overflowing, making her muscles pulse with sensation as he withdrew, then entered her again, each thrust deeper than the one before. She struggled to lift herself to her knees, wanting, needing the freedom to move. He helped her, then held her still as he thrust into her to the hilt again…and again. A deep moan made its way up from her abdomen and tore from her throat.

Again…again.

Yes….

Molly gave herself over gladly to the primitive emotion, plucking at every damn bit of frustration she'd encountered over the past two weeks and more, forming it into a tight ball, then throwing it away with force. She met him thrust for thrust. Holding steady when he needed her to and bearing back against him when it seemed he might pause. She curled her fingers into the top sheet, holding fast despite knowing that no physical action would be able to ground her against the wild storm building from within.

She felt his hand curve around her hip and slide toward her clit. She grasped his wrist, trying to stop him. She needed no more than feeling him inside her.

Then both their hands met over her delicate flesh, and they flew apart together.

# 13

YARDS AND YARDS OF cotton buffeted Molly as she slowly awakened. She felt as though she was floating, her body sated and throbbing. She felt gloriously complete.

Yet she sensed she was alone.

Opening her eyes, she was first aware of the all-encompassing darkness. She blinked until she could make out vague shapes. She'd been used to the light from the street in her hotel room, but here—she shivered—here, in Alan's place, everything was various shades of gray, with very little difference between them. Especially in the dark.

She heard the sound of a glass on a tabletop and lifted to her elbows. She'd known the instant she'd awakened that she was alone in the bed. But where was Alan?

She got up, grabbing his shirt from the floor and shrugging into it. She found him in the kitchen, sitting at the table alone in nothing but a pair of slacks left open at the waist. He was pouring himself a bourbon from one of the many bottles she'd seen around the apartment when she'd come in.

"Hey," she said quietly.

He seemed startled by her presence, so deep in thought he must not have heard her.

"Hey, yourself."

Molly wrapped her arms around her waist. She'd been around her share of drinkers. Her mother had gone on binges, usually over the weekend, when she wouldn't be working, but sometimes they'd carried into the next week, when she'd call in sick on Monday. But they'd usually passed quickly—although it had never seemed quick to Molly while her mother was going through it—and wrought no long-term effects. So long as she and Claire had steered a wide path around their mother, everything would usually be all right.

But over the past few days she'd gotten the impression that Alan's drinking went well beyond her mother's occasional binges usually brought about by a breakup. This…

This was something she felt well out of her depth to handle.

She swallowed hard. "Pour one for me?"

She made out his somber expression in the dim light coming in from the kitchen window. He got up, got a clean class from the cupboard and poured her a finger. She accepted the glass.

"Thanks."

She sipped the fiery liquor, fighting a shudder as its bitterness stung her tongue.

"You know…" she began, not thinking it smart to bring up his inability to sleep or his drinking, afraid he might show her the door. And for some reason she couldn't quite explain, she didn't want to go. She sensed that Alan, as fiercely independent as he was, needed company. Needed someone. And if that someone happened to be her…well, she couldn't just turn her back on him.

Didn't want to turn her back on him.

She pulled out the chair opposite him and sat down, bending her knee and hugging it to her chest. "Did I tell you I visited Claire's old apartment?" she said quietly. "I talked to her roommate. Asked her if maybe she'd remembered anything since she'd spoken to the police."

Alan sat holding his glass tightly, although he had yet to drink any of the contents since she'd appeared in the door.

Molly sipped her own drink, aware he hadn't indicated if he'd heard what she'd said.

She felt a tightness in her chest. An ache that looking at him amplified. He looked so raw, so alone, sitting there drinking in the dark.

She forged ahead on her own. "She was in the process of moving out—into her fiancé's place—and happened to come across something that belonged to Claire."

He finally looked at her.

Molly smiled, trying not to feel too relieved. "A key ring bearing a single key."

"It could belong to anyone."

Molly shook her head. "No. I know it's Claire's because I gave her the key ring myself for Christmas some time ago."

He didn't say anything for a long moment.

"I have no idea what it opens. I mean, it looks like it could be to a locker, but the plastic that might have held a number has been broken off."

He was looking at her now, although she couldn't make out his expression. But at least she had his attention.

"Do you think it opens anything important?"

"If it does, the odds of our finding out what it is are virtually nil."

Molly nodded. That was what she'd been afraid of. She'd visited the bus terminal yesterday morning and had been overwhelmed by the rows upon rows of lockers, some big, some small. She'd tried a couple of the lockers that were missing keys, but then she'd been weirded out by a homeless man following her even after she'd given him a couple bucks for a cup of coffee, and she'd left.

The utter silence of the room and the apartment around them was almost unsettling. Molly couldn't even make out the sound of a car passing, music playing. Nothing.

Nothing but the thick sound of her heart thudding against her rib cage.

She felt a connection to the man sitting across from her so intensely that it almost alarmed her. Especially since he was determined, for whatever godforsaken reason, to keep her at arm's length. Whether it be literally or with the help of a bourbon bottle.

At least he wouldn't have to drink alone so long as she was there.

She nudged her empty glass toward him. "Mind if I have a little more?"

He didn't respond for a long moment. Then he reached for the bottle and began opening it, before pushing it and the two glasses aside and reaching for her instead.

DAMN IT, BUT I COULDN'T help myself.

I knew I should tell Molly to leave. Knew I should fight the insatiable draw to her that burned in my gut hotter than the two shots of bourbon I'd had. But, damn me to hell, I couldn't do it.

I grabbed her by the shoulders and lifted her to the table so that she sat on it facing me. She gasped, soft strands of her hair caught in her lips as she stared up at me. I read part desire and part fear on her beautiful face as we stared at each other.

The past few hours with her had been incredible. I kept waiting for the point when I'd tire of her. Get my fill and want to push her away. But even when we were both spent and I'd drifted off to sleep, I'd known such a want for her that I'd awakened with a hard-on.

But rather than reaching for her, I'd headed for the kitchen.

And now here we both were.

I reached for the shirt she wore, finding it closed by only two buttons. I tugged, and the buttons ricocheted around the room, baring her to my gaze. I hungrily drank in her full breasts, weighing each in my right hand before squeezing almost to the point of pain.

She gasped.

I nudged my knee between hers, opening her thighs. The golden fleece between her legs glistened in the dim light.

I had no condoms on me. I stood looking down at the way her quickened breathing moved her breasts, causing her toned stomach to inflate and deflate. I listened to the sound of my own blood thickening, my erection so hard it was almost painful. Trailing my hand down from her breast to between her legs, I parted her engorged flesh and fit my uncovered tip against her opening, waiting for her to protest.

I heard the click of her swallow as she continued to stare at me.

I don't know how I knew that she was testing me, but I did.

I also knew that if I wanted to continue sans protection, she was opening the door for me to do so.

What kind of woman allowed that sort of sex in this day and age?

A woman too damn good for me.

I thrust my hands down under her buttocks and lifted her, then thrust into her to the hilt, knowing a sense of the dark and the forbidden. An untamed something within me that needed to claim her, to take advantage of her generosity, surged through my veins. A glass fell from the table and broke on the floor, the pieces stinging the top of my bare foot. I thrust again. And again. And the other glass and the bottle fell. But I was oblivious by then. Too far gone. I wanted to show Molly how I wasn't the guy for her. I was selfish and uncaring. I looked out only for my own gratification. I didn't want a woman like her in my life.

I wanted to chase her away.

But the harder I pushed, the harder she pushed back, giving as good as she got.

She braced her hands against the sides of the table and lifted her lush hips, meeting my angry thrusts stroke for stroke, her breasts swaying, her gaze plastered to mine. My thighs struck the side of the table again and again, and I knew I'd be bruised, that she'd be bruised, but I didn't care. In fact, I thought I'd welcome the visible reminder of just how wrong I was for her.

What type of man would purposely set out to hurt a woman as sweet and generous as Molly?

Her slick heat gripped me as she tightened her legs around my hips, her cry heralding her climax.

And as my own crisis built in the depth of my balls, I knew that the type of man who would do this was me. A man in need of something he was afraid only one woman could give him. Something he was afraid he'd never be good enough to receive....

WHEN MOLLY AWOKE HOURS later, she knew this time that she was not only alone in the bed but in the whole apartment. And as she sat up and drew her knees to her chest, she experienced what it felt like to be not only completely alone but utterly lonely.

ONE OF THE HARDEST things I'd ever done up until this point in my life was leave Molly as she lay in my bed this morning. Despite my strongest efforts to ward her off, the damnable woman was working her way under my skin. Reminding me of my own vulnerabilities. My own humanity.

My own need to touch and be touched.

But I found myself fighting her every step of the way, telling myself my reason for doing so had to do with my career—though I was beginning to suspect I wasn't ready to face the real reason.

So I'd left her lying there, her head against my pillow, looking like an angel.

But long before I'd received the call telling me of what had gone down, I'd been playing with something connected to the Arkart murder in my mind. Namely a piece of the puzzle that refused to fit.

Philippe Murrell.

The instant Molly had brought up his name, saying that she'd run into him outside Josie's hotel and that he hadn't seemed happy, an alarm had gone off in my mind. But I'd been too distracted at the time to act on it.

Perhaps if I had, I wouldn't be standing on Bourbon Street as the sun rose, watching NOFD try to put out the flames leaping from the fourth floor of the old hotel.

I scratched my jaw and turned toward where Josie herself was talking to Drew Morrison, her friend the tarot-card reader standing nearby. A cat meowed. I looked down to find a scruffy black cat staring up at me. Apparently having gotten what he wanted by gaining my attention, he flicked his tail, then scampered toward Josie.

"Sir, we're going to take the victim to New Orleans General now," a uniformed officer told me.

"He's a suspect, Jasper, not a victim."

I didn't care if Murrell had taken buckshot to the groin or not. If he had indeed murdered Frederique Arkart in a bid to get Josie to sell her hotel and gain himself a large paycheck from the same people Drew Morrison had been working for...well, he deserved a lot more than what Josie had given him.

I remembered the sawed-off shotgun behind her front desk and grimaced. Too bad she couldn't have aimed a little higher. There would have been less paperwork.

I walked toward my car, my presence unneeded since there weren't any murder victims and Arkart's killer had been caught. I should have felt better that I had one less murderer walking the city. And I did. To a certain degree anyway.

What I didn't feel good about was what I'd done to Molly last night.

I winced and pulled the car door open harder than I had to. After climbing inside, I sat for long moments before starting the engine.

Molly....

Well, Molly had proved she was made of sterner stuff than I'd given her credit for. Not only hadn't she turned away from the darkness that had unleashed itself during our lovemaking, she'd stared it straight in the face without blinking.

I wasn't too sure I was that courageous.

I turned the key in the ignition and put the car into gear. I wondered if she'd been awakened by the phone ringing an hour ago. Or whether she was still asleep in my bed.

I stopped for coffee and beignets, then headed for home. But when I opened the apartment door, I knew she was already long gone.

# 14

MOLLY HAD PURPOSELY kept out of touch with Alan since their night together. Not because she hadn't wanted to see him. But in spite of it.

It had been difficult to keep her distance. Every part of her had wanted to stay in his apartment the morning after, to wash up the few dishes in the sink, maybe make breakfast in case he returned.

Even though she'd surrendered herself to him in a way she never had with any man before him, she knew that to bend any more would be to risk snapping. And she couldn't do that.

No. If they were to go any further on a personal plane, Alan would have to be the one to take the next step. She knew that as surely as she knew her own name.

She also knew that he wouldn't respond immediately.

From the moment she'd first glanced into his deep green eyes, she'd guessed the dark detective was battling demons she couldn't begin to comprehend. But for a few brief hours Saturday night, she had glimpsed those demons from such a close proximity it had taken her breath away. She'd danced in that darkness, felt it swirling around her, sucking her in. And she'd willingly given herself over to the temptation of it. For Alan's sake.

For her sake.

But now she had to face that it was Monday morning and she hadn't heard from him. After a long Sunday at the hotel, going over notes and files and her sister's things while waiting for the phone to ring or someone to knock at her door, she was beginning to fear that he wouldn't make the next move. That he would stay in the shadows and not reach out for her.

Straightening her skirt, she stood a little straighter and told herself she'd known the consequences of her actions.

But that didn't make Alan's silence go down any easier.

She lifted her hand and knocked at the door to a nice middle-class home that seemed to be on the fence between the city and the surrounding bayous. It opened immediately.

"I'm sorry I'm late," Molly said to FBI agent Akela Brooks.

"Don't worry about it. I don't have to be anywhere until ten." She motioned for Molly to follow her down a hall.

Molly noticed the agent looked flushed and happy.

The apparent reason for her state stepped up behind her in the kitchen, tall and forbidding-looking.

"Molly, this is Claude Lafitte. Claude…Molly."

Molly stretched out her hand, amazed by how large the Cajun was.

"*Mon dieu,* you look exactly like Claire," he said quietly—and none too discreetly in front of his fiancée. After all, he'd spent the night with her sister before she'd been found dead the following morning in the bed they'd shared.

His eyes narrowed and he shook a long, thick finger at her. "Then again, maybe not. There is something different about you, isn't there?"

Molly wasn't sure an answer was expected from her, so she didn't offer one.

"Please, have a seat," Akela said. "Coffee?"

"Please."

Molly sat down, noticing that Claude chose to lean against a counter nearer the back door rather than sit.

"Never mind him," Akela said as she poured the coffee. "He still feels hunted. Being near the door gives him a quick escape route."

Molly's gaze went back to the Cajun. "I see."

Although she really didn't. She couldn't imagine living always under suspicion, always on the run. And it intrigued her that as an FBI agent, Akela was the one who usually did the suspecting and the hunting.

Two halves of the same whole? She watched as Claude took the coffeepot from Akela, his fingers subtly lingering on hers. Molly dropped her gaze at the obvious look of love they exchanged, feeling like a Peeping Tom even though she was an invited guest.

"Thanks so much for agreeing to see me," she said, clearing her throat and taking out her notes. "I trust you both have heard about Hotel Josephine."

"Yes," Akela said.

"The copycat killing has rolled back attention to the first murder—that of your sister," Claude said, with deference, "which means I'm also back in the spotlight."

"That's why I thought it might be a good idea for us to meet," Molly said. "So I can share what new information I have." She smiled. "And perhaps convince you to share with me the evidence that points in another direction…."

She left her words purposely hanging, watching as the two shared a knowing glance.

"Okay, what do you got?" Claude asked, folding his arms across his impressive chest, while Akela took a seat across the table from her.

"First," Molly said, pulling out Claire's diary, "I've been reading this since I got my sister's personal belongings from you, Akela." She flipped open to a passage of interest. "Here she says that 'C'…" Molly didn't know if she had to explain who "C" was.

Akela nodded. "The married man Claire had been seeing."

"Right. Anyway, here she mentions that 'C' tried

to take the diary away from her. Which means—" she carefully closed it with the bookmark in it "—that C's fingerprints might be on the diary itself."

Akela frowned. "A lot of people have handled that diary, Molly."

"That's what I was afraid you were going to say."

"Even if I were to get the FBI forensics team to lift an original fingerprint, the odds that we could use it are slim. After I handed it over to you, there's no identifiable chain of custody. Then there's the period before that, when her roommate, Joann, had it."

Molly put the diary back into the clear Ziploc bag she'd stored it in. "Okay."

"Is that it?" Claude asked.

Molly smiled at him. "No." She pulled out the key chain Alan hadn't taken much of an interest in. "I happened by Claire's old apartment while her ex-roommate was moving out. She found this."

Akela took it. "Are you sure it belonged to your sister?"

"Positive."

She was intrigued that Akela didn't question her further. Merely accepted her statement as fact.

"Do you know what it opens?" Claude asked, taking the key and squinting at it.

"Not a clue. I went to the bus station the other morning but the task seems too enormous. Do you think you can do anything with it?"

Akela looked at her over the key. "Maybe. At

the very least, we can narrow down where it originates from."

"Wait," Molly said, taking the key from her before she could pocket it. "You don't need the ring, do you?"

"No."

She removed the key and handed it back to the agent, then squeezed the tiny troll in her palm.

A cacophony of sound started from somewhere upstairs, then continued down what Molly could only gather were the stairs. Within seconds a girl of about four or five burst into the room wreathed in giggles, five pups on her heels.

"Save me, save me, Claude!" the girl squealed, lifting her arms.

Claude scooped her up, and one of the puppies had a hard time stopping on the tiled floor, skidding into the Cajun's shins.

Akela was shaking her head across from Molly. "This is my daughter, Daisy. And the puppies… well, they and their mother essentially came with the house. Meaning they were camped out on the back porch."

Molly patted one of their heads and instantly found herself accosted by all five. The black pups with white spots looked like a mix of border collie and golden retriever, with border collie winning out.

What had to be the mother's toenails clicked in the hall. She stuck her nose into the room, sniffed, then barked. All five of the rambunctious pups fell over each other to get to her. Claude put a suddenly squirming Daisy down to follow.

"Daisy, go wash up," Akela said. "The bus gets here in twenty minutes."

"Aw, Mom," the girl protested, then chased the dogs from the room.

Claude chuckled. "You wouldn't happen to be in the market for a dog, would you, Molly?"

She reluctantly shook her head. "Sorry, no. Before too long I'll be heading back to Toledo, and I don't think my condo neighbors would be very happy if I brought one of these home with me."

The reality that soon she'd be leaving New Orleans dampened the high spirits raised by the girl and the puppies. She didn't appreciate the cards fate had dealt her. She was here to help find her sister's killer. But the instant she did that, she would have to leave the city—and Alan—behind.

"So," she said, taking a deep breath and looking at Akela and Claude. "Your turn."

"LOOKS LIKE YOU'RE having a hard time over there, Chevalier."

I slanted a glare at one of the junior detectives in Vice as I negotiated the rolling path from hell that was the treadmill. I hadn't realized how long it had been since I'd worked out until I'd gotten on the damn thing, set the pace, then found myself huffing and puffing a minute into my workout. This, and I'd long since stopped smoking.

"You need someone to spot you?"

I grimaced and slowed the pace, deciding my best course of action was to ignore the pain in the ass. That, and I was afraid of how I might sound if I did speak. A rasped threat didn't hold the same weight somehow.

Three miles. Damn. There was a time when I could have easily run ten. But that had been almost a year ago, and I was essentially going from a flat-out stop to a full-out run. I was lucky I had a naturally athletic physique—a lean build, a tight stomach—or I would have only Jell-O for muscles right now. I pulled the towel from the handle and draped it over my neck, using the end to wipe the sweat dripping from my forehead. I smelled the bleached white cloth, half surprised my sweat didn't hold the scent of bourbon. I grabbed my water bottle and downed half the contents, looking at my watch as I did.

Only nine o'clock.

The time since I'd left Molly sleeping in my bed alone yesterday morning had been torture. I'd driven past her hotel no fewer than five times the night before, trying to make out which room would be hers in the countless windows facing the street, gripping the steering wheel tightly in case I'd be tempted to get out and go up to her.

Instead I'd driven to a nearby church where I knew an AA meeting took place three nights a week,

Sunday being one of them. A kind of pep talk for the week ahead. I'd gone in, taken a seat in the back and watched without participating.

You see, what my ex-wife didn't know was that I'd not only been to the meeting before, I was a full-fledged member. Had joined during that time when she'd noticed that I would spend night after night locked in what had once been my father's office, the library of the house.

Oh, I knew the rules well. And that was when I'd taken up smoking, trading one bad habit for another. Although while both would chase me to an early grave, cigarettes wouldn't get me arrested for DUI or make me a target for MADD or get me fired from my job.

Thankfully I'd been able to quit cigarettes without joining another group that would get me hooked on Mrs. Fields cookies or something.

At any rate, I hadn't been to a meeting in more than five years, and it had been strange sitting there listening to the others' stories.

Had I really fallen back that far?

Yes, I realized, I had.

And the reality hit in me in the stomach like a sucker punch.

I'd recognized a couple of the guys there, and one had come up to me midway through the session, before I could duck out.

"Hey, Alan," Tom had said, sitting next to me. Part of the process involved being sponsored by someone in the group when you were new and then returning the favor and advancing further on down the path to sobriety by becoming a sponsor later. I'd sponsored Tom. And was a little surprised to find him still there.

"Relapse?" he asked me.

"Somewhat. You?"

"No. I come every now and again just to remind myself that even a glass of wine can lead me right back to where I was. And I sponsor every now and again."

Tom had come from a long family of drinkers and had hit the bottle hard when his wife and kids had left him. Not only had he stopped drinking, but he'd reconciled with his wife. An all-around success story.

I'd looked down at my wrinkled clothes and wondered what that made me.

Which is why I was now running myself through the ringer at the gym around the corner from the precinct.

Well, I was using the word *running* loosely. In reality, I was walking really fast.

I stepped off the treadmill, then headed for the showers. I didn't kid myself into thinking it would be easy pushing the bottle aside for a second time. But I had to start somewhere.

I was in the locker room putting my stuff away in my bag when my cell phone rang.

I didn't recognize the number on the display.

"You are screwing your ex again," came Astrid's scathing indictment.

I sighed. "How in the hell did you get my direct cell number?"

"From one of your sisters."

I stiffened. I didn't like the thought of Astrid being in contact with members of my family.

As for her accusation, I admit, for the first couple of years after Val and I split, we'd get together for what we called "ex sex." Essentially they'd been one-night liaisons designed to relieve stress with someone we already knew we liked and had great sex with. That had stopped about three years ago, though, when we'd decided that constant intimacy might put our friendship in jeopardy. And neither of us had been willing to risk that.

"You didn't answer my question," she said.

"I wasn't aware you'd asked one."

"Are you sleeping with your ex?"

I remembered that day ten months ago when I'd given myself over to lust and bedded Astrid. As we'd lain in bed afterward, she'd asked about my ex, and I'd answered, telling her that we'd slept together from time to time but that there was no passionate love there.

Now, just as then, I felt compelled to answer her. While I couldn't claim any real lasting emotion for her, the truth wouldn't hurt if it provided her relief. "No, Astrid. I'm not."

Shortly thereafter, she hung up.

Christ. When I'd acknowledged that giving up the

bottle would be difficult, I hadn't factored in situations like the one with Astrid. I hefted my gym bag and headed for the door to see what other problems fate had lined up for me, personally and professionally.

# 15

MOLLY SAT AT THE FAR end of the bar at the Gas Lantern later that night, again waiting for Alan. Their agreement was that they would meet there regularly at nine until her sister's killer was found. She glanced at her watch. Only it didn't look as though Alan intended to keep up his end of the bargain.

Again.

She took a deep breath. He hadn't made the last meeting, and she'd gone to his apartment. She didn't think it was a good idea to do that again, for obvious reasons. No matter how loudly her body and heart protested.

She shifted uncomfortably on the stool, glad the place was quiet tonight, the band replaced by a jukebox.

Alan had never been easy to read. Her first impressions of him when she'd spoken to him on the phone from Toledo hadn't been favorable. He'd stonewalled her, shut her out. And he'd begun to do the same when she'd met with him for the first time down here. But now...well, the puzzle pieces she was beginning to collect from several different people were forming a picture that only made him all the more enigmatic.

It had begun when Claude had asked about Alan before sharing the evidence that pointed away from Claude, namely surveillance footage of a black-cloaked mystery woman—or small man—coming out of the Josephine moments after the estimated time of Claire's murder.

*How well do you know Detective Chevalier?* Claude had asked.

For a reason she had yet to fathom, she'd felt curiously uncomfortable under the scrutiny of his intense gaze. She'd suspected he'd known of her growing feelings for Alan, no matter how impossible that had seemed. Put it down to a guy thing maybe, but she was convinced he'd known more than he was sharing. Maybe in the course of their own investigation, he and Akela had picked up on her and Alan's connection.

With that question out of the way, they'd then shared a few pieces of information about Alan that she hadn't wanted to believe but had known were true just the same. Not just because she trusted Akela. But because they just…fit.

She thought about the man she'd seen in the picture with his three sisters. She now knew he'd become entangled with his supervising captain's estranged wife, which had put the captain on a mission to see Alan fired. Add that he had arrested the wrong man, by way of Claude, for Claire's murder and…

Well, you got the man she knew now.

"The guy ought to be taken out back and taught a lesson," the bartender, Jack Cadieux, said, freshening her drink even though she hadn't asked him to.

She smiled at him, reminding herself that he didn't know what she'd been thinking. "I take it knowing exactly the right thing to say comes with owning a bar."

He chuckled. "You could say that. Although in this case, I mean it. Leaving a pretty woman like you sitting waiting all by yourself has to be a crime somewhere in the world."

She sighed. "Unfortunately not here."

Another customer came in and Jack moved down the bar to serve him.

Molly watched the exchange, wondering what she should do next. Go back to the hotel? She thought of the diary she still had in her bag, along with the key-ring troll, and knew that she didn't want to go back to her room just yet. She'd rather wait around here, even if the spotlight of stood-up woman was shining on her.

Yes, she knew that her heart played a huge role in her growing attachment to the mysterious detective. Maybe because not much time had passed since she'd lost her twin sister and her emotions were close to the surface, her heart exposed and vulnerable. Definitely because something within him reached out to her in a way that she couldn't ignore, much less refuse.

"C!"

She snapped upright to find Jack shouting out the greeting to someone who'd just walked in. In more ways than one, she was surprised to find it was Alan.

JACK PUT DOWN MY USUAL bourbon bottle and clean glass in front of me when I walked down the bar to stand next to Molly.

"Sorry, Jack, not tonight," I said.

While Molly had yet to wear another dress similar to the little red number I'd seen her in the other night, she still captured my attention in a way that set off alarms. And not only on a sexual level. Whenever I was with her I felt...whole somehow, even though I'd never considered myself empty.

"You look...different," she said quietly.

I glanced down at my new shirt and pressed slacks, then rubbed my freshly shaved jaw. "Not so you wouldn't recognize me on the street," I said.

My overcoat was still creased and wrinkled. That, I couldn't help. Not until I could buy a replacement, because I wasn't willing to wait even an hour while it was dry-cleaned. Not now. Not in the middle of an important investigation.

"I don't know," she said. "I'm reasonably sure I would have passed you without a second glance."

I stared at her.

She motioned with her hands. "I didn't mean that the way it came out." She nudged her glass around in a circle in front of her. Bourbon. But it looked like she hadn't touched it.

My mouth watered.

"Come on," I said, grabbing my hat from where I'd put it on the bar. "Let's go someplace else."

She blinked her pretty blues at me, and I motioned for her to lead the way out. Partly because that's what a gentleman did for a lady. Mostly because it gave me a grade-A view of her backside.

If it also prevented her from looking at me too closely, that was between me and the wall.

Truth was, I wasn't all that keen on her thinking she was responsible for the changes I was making to my life. Although it might come a little closer to the truth than I was comfortable with. I mean, if I hadn't met Molly Laraway, would I now be back at the gym and refusing a glass of bourbon? Or would Val's talking to me have been enough?

No. I knew that all roads to where I currently stood began with Molly. Mostly because I hadn't liked the man I saw through her eyes. In the beginning, I'd tried to stave off my attraction to her to save myself the trouble. But once we'd crossed the line and I'd gotten a really good look at myself back at my place…well, I knew I had to make a few changes, but quick. If only so I could live with myself.

"You look good," she said, walking next to me.

Nowhere was the *click-click* of her heels against the promenade, because she wore flats rather than stilettos. But she was woman enough that she didn't need the props.

"Thanks," I said, rubbing my chin again. My skin itched. It wasn't used to being without the stubble, and I imagined it putting up a protest.

"Here," I said, opening the door to a coffee shop.

She entered and motioned toward a table near the front. I instead led her toward the back, where we both sat, me with my eye on the door.

"I thought you might not come."

I grimaced. "Sorry. I got caught up with a lead on Zoe."

"Your sister?"

I nodded. "Yeah. I got a line on the kid Frankenstein said she's dating." If her brief smile was anything to go by, she caught my reference to the bartender at the Goth bar. "I stopped by to talk to his parents. He hasn't been home for the same length of time Zoe's been missing."

*Missing.* I hated saying that word. It implied too much.

And I was starting to worry.

Molly nodded. Clearly she was preoccupied. I thought I knew her well enough to see that.

Of course, it would stand to reason that she might be feeling a little uneasy herself. After all, we'd slept together. And I hadn't called. Worse, I was not only acting like it hadn't happened, I'd been late for our regular meeting.

"You okay?" I found myself asking and cringed.

That was a dangerous question for a man to ask. I'd walked the earth long enough to know that. Still, for some stupid reason, I'd asked it.

She blinked at me and I braced myself for recriminations.

"Why did Jack call you 'C' back at the Gas Lantern?"

Whoa. Not exactly what I'd been expecting.

Not that I'd been expecting anything.

I cleared my throat. "Jack often calls me 'C.' He does that with a lot of his customers, shortens their last name to the first initial." I put my hat on the table. "Frankly I think it's because he wants to cover his ass should anyone come up on some kind of most-wanted list. Plausible deniability."

I'd been trying to be funny. But Molly wasn't smiling.

Then it hit me. Her sister had referred to the man she'd been seeing as "C" in her diary.

"You're not implying what I think you are?" I asked, sitting back in my chair.

I mean, what kind of man did she take me for?

The type of man who would selfishly bang her, then leave her hanging in the morning.

She shook her head and sighed. "I'm sorry. I'm not implying anything. I guess all this—" she looked around "—is starting to get to me."

Just as she was starting to get to me in all the

ways a man fears a woman getting to him. A way that made him want to move heaven and earth in order to please her.

"Yeah," I said. "Maybe it's getting to us both."

I ordered two coffees to go from the waitress.

"So is there anything you want to share about what happened at the hotel yesterday?" she asked.

I felt like a heel that I hadn't been the one to tell her. "It pretty much went down the way the news reported it. Philippe Murrell was the copycat killer."

I didn't know if she was aware she was rubbing her arms. "I can't believe it's the same guy I talked to outside the hotel."

"You probably weren't in any danger. Philippe's intentions were situational."

"Meaning he killed to try to get Josie to sell the hotel."

"Meaning that, yes."

"Strange way to go about it."

"I don't think he's in possession of all of his marbles."

Our coffees were brought to the table. I took the lid off mine and began pouring sugar inside.

"Like a little coffee with your sugar?" Molly asked.

I grimaced and let up.

"Do you want some?" I asked.

She shook her head, added cream to hers, then put the lid back on. "There's one thing I was hoping you could do for me."

Uh-oh. Here we go.

She reached to take something out of her purse. I recognized the diary of her sister through the plastic bag. The same diary in which Claire had mentioned that a married guy named "C" was her lover.

"In the place I have marked, Claire mentions something about 'C' trying to physically take the diary from her."

I accepted the diary before I could consider that maybe it wasn't a good idea. "And you think his fingerprints might be on it."

"Yes. I mean, I know that it's been handled a lot since Claire died, but if there's even a remote chance that the killer's prints are on there—"

"And are in our system."

She held my gaze. "No stone unturned and all that."

I nodded. It was the least I could do, I supposed, after my behavior over the past couple of days.

I sat back.

She gathered her things and began to get up. "Was there anything else?"

I blinked several times. "I didn't have anything."

"Good. So we'll meet in two days? Would you prefer here?"

I nodded.

She didn't comment but paused for a long moment, as if waiting for me to say something. But for the life of me, I couldn't imagine what she wanted me to say.

"Good night, Alan."

"Um, yeah. Good night."

Then I sat there like an idiot and watched her walk out of the coffee shop. What else should I have done?

# 16

MOLLY RETURNED TO HER hotel room. She didn't know what she'd expected. No, *expected* wasn't the word exactly. Rather, she'd *hoped* that Alan would make some sort of definitive move one way or another at the coffee shop when she'd risen to leave.

She closed her hotel room door behind her. Actually, he had made a move, hadn't he? By not objecting to her leaving or suggesting perhaps she stay or that they go somewhere else, he was telling her that what had happened the other night had been a one-time deal. A brief night of sex.

She picked up her purse and walked the rest of the way into the room, switching on lights, then tossing her purse to a nearby armchair. Hey, she was an adult. She'd had sex without the promise of more before. She could deal with it now.

Or could she?

"Don't be stupid," she said to herself aloud, hoping the sound of her voice would snap her out of her melancholy mood.

When that didn't work, she switched on the TV,

flipping through a series of talking heads and commentators, movies and sitcoms, then pressing mute and turning on the radio instead. The tinny, mellow sound of the blues filled the room through the small speaker. She stretched across the bed and stared at the ceiling.

And she *was* stupid, wasn't she? What exactly had she expected? Or even hoped for? A liaison with the handsome detective to last the length of her stay in the Crescent City?

Her mind froze on that thought. And he truly was handsome, wasn't he? He had been since the beginning, but tonight…tonight she'd wanted to order him up from the menu. She'd felt the almost irresistible desire to lick his smooth jawline. Run her fingers through his neatly trimmed hair. Bury her nose in the crisp fabric of his shirt before kissing his clean-smelling neck.

She took a deep breath, then slowly exhaled. Sex. That was all she'd been looking for. To want anything more would be unrealistic. Alan was New Orleans to a tee. She planned on returning to Toledo. What future was there in that kind of relationship?

None.

The telephone rang on the bedside table. She lay still for a moment, almost afraid to hope that Alan might be calling her. Then she scrambled for the receiver, nearly dropping it before pulling it to her ear.

"Hello?"

"Molly? Jesus, girl, is that you?"

Her mother.

She was of half a mind to hang up on her, she was so disappointed it wasn't Alan. "Hi, Mom."

"You mean you're still there? I thought for sure you would have come home with your tail between your legs by now."

"They haven't caught Claire's killer yet."

"And what does that have to do with you?"

How did she explain it in a way that made sense to her mother? Hell, how did she explain it in a way that made sense to *her?*

"I've already told you why I need to be down here, Mom. Please don't make me do it again."

"Okay, I won't. If only because I don't want to pay any more for the call than I have to."

That was Mom for you, forever budget-minded. "Was there something you wanted?"

She sighed heavily. "That's just like you and your sister. Treating me with disrespect."

"I do not disrespect you, Mom." She reached for her purse and fished out the troll key ring. She rubbed the pad of her thumb against the ink across the plastic face.

"Yes, you do. And so did your sister. I mean, just what the hell am I supposed to do with a box I can't open?"

Molly's heart skipped a beat as she rose to her elbows. "Box?"

"Yes, box. Your sister sent me this metal box about three months ago. Told me to keep it for her."

"What's in it?"

"Didn't I just say it was locked?"

She'd said she couldn't open it.

"I've tried just about every damn thing. Even asked the locksmith to open it for me, but when I told him it was Claire's, he asked to see papers showing I'd inherited it. Can you believe it?"

Molly smiled. Funny how her aggravating mother ran into problems like that all the time. Fate's way of paying her back for her transgressions, she guessed.

"Mom, I want you to send the box to me. Overnight mail."

"Why?"

"Because I think I have the key."

Well, she didn't physically have the key at that moment. Akela had it. But she could get it.

"Well, if you have the key, send it to me."

"Mom, can you please just do as I ask?"

There was a long pause. "What if there's money in there?"

Molly rolled her eyes and pressed her fingertips to her aching temples. "I'll make sure you get every cent," she promised.

"You know how much it'll cost me to mail this thing? Especially overnight?"

"Take it to my office and give it to my assistant. She'll send it to me."

That was a better alternative yet. She could imagine her mother going to the post office, hearing what it would cost to send the package overnight and sending it third class instead.

At any rate, it would be the day after tomorrow before she'd see the package. So long as her mother got it to the office before nine tomorrow morning. Which she promised she would after Molly vowed to wire her any money she found inside.

Molly decided she'd wait to find out if the key could indeed open the box's lock. She had a strong suspicion that it would. If it had been a simple lock, her mother would have had no trouble opening the box. That she'd called in a locksmith was promising.

There was a light knock at the door.

She sat up. She had been thinking about ordering room service since she'd eaten only a bagel and cream cheese for breakfast and nothing else. She'd hoped that Alan might want to catch a bite.

Alan.

She got up from the bed, smoothed the covers, then stepped to look through the peephole. Sure enough, there he was, looking as good as sin and twice as tempting.

I KNEW SHE WAS IN THERE. I'd heard her talking on the phone when I'd neared the door. Since she'd said "Mom," I knew she'd been speaking to her mother.

I took off my hat, then ran a hand through my hair.

Hell, I wouldn't blame her if she didn't answer. I'd let her walk out of that coffee shop like it wasn't any never mind to me what she did with her time. And even, perhaps, like she was wasting mine. Which couldn't be further from the truth.

"Alan," she said.

I hadn't realized she'd opened the door until I heard her say my name.

Women. They sure knew how to make a man feel crazy just by whispering in a certain way.

No, not all women. This woman knew how to speak in a way that made me crazy.

"May I come in?"

She seemed almost as knocked off center as I was. "Um, sure. Yes. Come in. Please."

I passed her and stood in the middle of the room that looked homier than my place, even though I'd been there for more than five years and she only a few days. Bottles of lotion were on the nightstand, papers and a laptop were on the desk, a newspaper was on a chair beside her purse and the television looked like it belonged in this century.

"Has something happened?" she said, standing next to me.

"Happened? Oh, you mean on the case. No, no. Nothing new."

But something had happened with me.

Something important.

Because after she'd walked out of that shop, I'd

realized how much I wanted—almost needed—to be with her.

"Oh. Okay. Um, would you like me to order up something from room service? Coffee? Or I think the minibar might have something…."

She crouched down to break the seal on the small refrigerator and looked around inside.

"A Coke ought to do it."

She looked at the small bottles of liquor she'd taken out, placed them back inside and grabbed the cola.

"I'll just go, um, get some ice," she said.

She grabbed the bucket out of the bathroom, then stepped out into the hall, leaving me alone in the room.

I moved to the desk and eyed the papers spread across the top. Most of them I was familiar with. A couple of items I wasn't. I picked up a small picture frame holding a shot of Molly with her sister, both of them smiling into the camera. Interestingly I found I could instantly tell the difference between the two. Claire was laughing almost too hard, posing for the camera, while Molly had a warmth and intelligence and subtle sexiness that spoke to the picture taker and reached out to me even from the inanimate photo.

I put the frame back down when I heard the door open.

Within moments she'd filled two glasses with ice and poured the Coke, handing me one.

"Please, sit," she said, indicating the armchair.

She took her purse and the newspaper off it, then sat down on the bed.

I sat on the chair.

And felt even dumber than I had at the coffee shop.

"So," she said, obviously not feeling any better than I did. "What do we do next?"

I squinted at her. Surely she wasn't asking what I wanted to do? Because what I wanted to do was join her on that king-size bed.

"I mean with the case," she said, apparently catching on to the suggestive nature of her question.

"Ah, the case. Yes." I sipped the Coke, then put it down and wiped my hand on the front of my coat before placing the hat I held in my other hand on the desk. "I drove the diary downtown. Steven—that would be Steven Chan, the chief of forensics—won't be in until tomorrow, but I left it there for him so he can take a look at it first thing."

She nodded. "Thanks." Her head snapped up from where she was looking at the glass she held. "Should I have my fingerprints taken? You know, so they can be ruled out as the killer's?"

"That's a good idea. Come on down to the station tomorrow and I'll have one of the booking agents take care of it."

She nodded again.

Then a silence ensued that I didn't know quite what to do with.

It wasn't often that I was in this type of situation.

And while I didn't like it, I liked the alternative—leaving—even less. I'd rather be here and uncomfortable than away from Molly and wanting to be with her.

She smiled. "Talk about your awkward silences."

I smiled back. Then I leaned forward, joining my hands between my knees. "Molly, look…"

I'd started talking, but I didn't really know what I wanted to say. Nothing and everything. Which could mean we could be there all night.

"I just wanted to say that my last intention is to hurt you."

She bent her legs so that her bare feet hugged the edge of the bed. "Who said you'd hurt me?"

"Your body language, for one."

She looked at her knees.

"I'd never thought it a good idea for us to get involved."

"We had sex, Alan. We're not involved."

"Ah, but that's where you're wrong."

She cocked her head, causing the highlights in her hair to shift under the lamplight.

"You see, while I told myself that the reason we shouldn't get involved—or become intimate, if that's the description you'd prefer—was that we were working on this case together, the truth is I always knew, sensed really, that whatever happened between us would be more than just about…"

"The sex?"

"Yes."

She stretched her legs back out to hang over the side of the bed. "What are you trying to say, Alan?"

I grimaced. "You're not going to make this easy on me, are you?"

The ghost of a smile. "Not a chance."

I considered myself blessed that I was surrounded by smart women. I also considered myself cursed. Because not only couldn't I get away with lying to them, they wouldn't let me lie to myself, either. Which was a major drawback.

"Let's just say that I'm coming to feel something for you that's well beyond a physical urge."

"Urge?"

"Intense need for you…physically."

She leaned her weight back on her arms against the bed, stretching out her torso. I gazed at her breasts and her narrow hips, then back up into her face. "And you're feeling that need now?"

Was I ever.

"Show me."

# 17

NOW THAT WAS MORE invitation than any twenty men could refuse.

And I wasn't about to refuse it.

I stood up, shrugged out of my overcoat and laid it across the chair. Then I unbuttoned the cuffs of my new shirt and tugged the hem out of the waist of my pants, my gaze fused with hers while I stepped out of my shoes. She seemed intrigued by my actions. But if she'd been hoping for a full Monty, she wasn't getting it. Instead I sat on the bed next to her, hip to hip, thigh to thigh, and stared at her.

God, but she was beautiful. Especially when she was trying to work something out and couldn't quite seem to wrap her mind around it. I watched as her tongue dipped out and moistened her lips, her pulse visible at the base of her neck.

"May I?" I asked.

The click of her swallow sounded above the soft blues playing on the radio. She nodded.

I reached out and touched her hair. So silky. So pretty.

"I thought you were asking for permission to kiss me," she whispered.

"No, Molly. I've done enough taking. From here on out, everything between us happens because you've made it happen."

"So," she rasped, "you're saying if I want you to get closer to me, I have to get closer to you?"

I nodded, watching as she shifted so that her face was closer to mine.

"And that if I want you to kiss me, I should kiss you?"

I moved to nod again, then stopped when she leaned in, placing her lips gently against mine. I groaned and threaded my fingers through her hair so that they lay against her head. I kissed her back.

Sweet Jesus, she was incredible. I kept thinking that if I tried hard enough to find a way to have her yet keep her away at the same time, I would find one. But she refused me that luxury, demanding all or nothing.

And for me, *nothing* was no longer an option.

As a recovering alcoholic, I knew the dangers of substituting one addiction for another. Smoking instead of drinking, for example. And as I kissed—just kissed—Molly, I knew the fear that I was replacing bourbon with her. While on the surface that might not seem so bad, below I knew that by attaching myself to her, I was giving up control. And the program taught control, step-by-step, day by day, as the first stride in regaining ownership of your life.

But how was a man supposed to tell the difference between addiction and…love?

Molly slid her tongue against mine and heat traveled all over my body. She tasted sweet and so damn good I couldn't seem to get enough of her, the sensations far more potent than anything that a bottle could offer.

Love….

Didn't love also demand that you surrender all sense of control? If so, how was that different from addiction? Was there a pill you could take? A program you could enter? A group you could join?

I trailed my fingertips down to the shell of her ear, then lower still to where her pulse pounded in her delicate throat.

I knew love. Familial love. And surely I'd loved—and still loved—my ex. I'd sacrifice my life for her and my sisters in order to keep them safe. I'd give everything I had to make sure they were clothed and fed and healthy. They hurt, I hurt. No matter what was on my agenda, I'd always have time for them.

But what I felt for Molly now went well beyond all that. It was overwhelming and all-encompassing. I felt her under my skin, in my veins, as if somehow the impossible had happened and we had become one. One in mind and heart.

She pressed her hand against my chest, not to push me away but rather to probe the muscles under my shirt. Her touch seemed to brand me in a way I feared and hoped would last forever. Though forever might be defined as this one night. Because one thing I'd learned in my lifetime was that everything could change within the blink of an eye.

Which made it that much more important that I do exactly as Molly asked and show her how I felt.

NOT ONLY DID ALAN LOOK different, he was different.

Molly cracked open her eyelids, viewing him through the hazy cloud of emotion that seemed to emanate from him to her. Gone was the savage expression he'd worn the other night, as if he'd needed to claim her in a way that demanded she bend to his will. In its place was a gentle coaxing, a sharing that made her heart expand in her chest. And the longing she felt was for more than sexual need. It was for an intangible something that you couldn't wrap up but that was a gift nonetheless. Perhaps the greatest gift of all.

A connection that only love could form.

"I want to see you," he murmured, breaking their kiss and slipping his fingers to the front of her blouse. He began undoing the buttons. Molly was helpless to do anything but watch. Not his actions, but his face. There was a calmness about him. A sense that he was not only in touch with the way he felt but that he wasn't afraid to show those feelings to her. When he finished opening her blouse, his eyes gazed into hers again. And in them she saw a warm smile and deep desire.

And that turned her on more than any words and touched her more than any caress.

She returned the favor, sliding out each of the buttons down the front of his shirt until she could slowly push the cotton from his shoulders, revealing every hard inch of his abs, every smooth muscle. She leaned forward and pressed her lips and nose against his right shoulder. He smelled of soap. And tasted of him as she ran her tongue over his skin, following the dampness with openmouthed kisses.

Without her being entirely aware, he stripped her of her bra and her pants, leaving only her panties. Then she went about seeing that he also shed his clothes, including his boxers.

The physical proof of his need for her stood ramrod straight. But as she wrapped her fingers around the molten thickness, she absorbed his emotional need for her in the green depths of his eyes. He seemed to be holding his breath, fighting against something she was causing. Not only physically, but emotionally.

He gently gripped her shoulders and urged her to lie back against the pillows. She didn't fight him. And when she felt his mouth at her breast, her throat tightened, every lap of his tongue against her taut nipple sending ripples of pleasure over her belly. Such sweet pleasure. Then, as if he was following the path of those ripples, he traced a path down her quivering stomach. He paused there, as if surprised by her vulnerable reaction, and looked up into her face.

Never in her life had Molly felt so exposed to another human being. Instinct tempted her to look away. But she fought to hold his gaze, answering whatever question he was asking with honesty.

His thumbs hooked either side of her panties, and she expected him to release her from the intensity of his gaze. Instead he continued holding her captive as his mouth followed the edge of her descending panties, millimeter by millimeter, until his tongue found the tight bud nestled in her curls.

Molly gasped, her hips coming up off the sheets as lightning crackled through her body.

Still she somehow managed to maintain eye contact as Alan skimmed her panties down her legs, then off completely. Unlike their coming together a couple of nights before, there was no rush now. No overpowering urgency. Rather Molly felt as though her bones were long-burning embers waiting, waiting to be fanned back into flame. And that moment loomed so very far away yet so very near as Alan slowly slid his hands over her legs, from the outside to the inside, then back again, until they rested firmly against her inner thighs and paused there.

One heartbeat...two heartbeats...

Molly spread her legs.

She felt rather than heard Alan's groan. It flowed over her skin, around and around, inspiring a shiver that vibrated every part of her body. His thumbs traced the line of her crevice, then he parted her swollen flesh. Molly twisted her fingers into the sheets at the first fiery flick of his tongue against her hood. Her heartbeat quadrupled in her chest, yet she still felt languid, incapable of movement. Another flick, then a pad of a thumb against the button. Her hips instinctively bucked.

"No, Molly, don't close your eyes," he murmured as he held her still with his hands.

She swallowed thickly just before he fastened his mouth over the most delicate part of her. It took everything in her power not to close her eyes as her shivers exploded into muscle-deep shudders, the only thing keeping her anchored Alan's mouth against her as she climaxed.

She fully expected him to move from between her thighs when the spasms stopped. Instead he slowly laved her, lapping up the evidence of her climax… and creating an even more intense need deep within her.

By the time he finally kissed his way up her stomach, Molly felt as if she'd melted completely against the bed, nothing but a puddle of need. He licked her hypersensitive nipples, then nuzzled her neck before his hips came to rest between her legs.

I'D NEVER SEEN A WOMAN look so beautiful.

Molly Laraway was everything—and more than—a man could ever wish for. Beyond her obvious physical attributes there was a warmth and generosity about her. And a trust that made me feel protective of her, watchful over her and one with her all at once.

And I wanted to please her in a way that I'd never wanted to please anyone before her.

I framed her face with my hands, smoothing back her hair and staring into her blue, blue eyes. Her climax moments before had been so powerful that it had taken all I had not to follow right along with her, without touch, without penetration. I was so tuned in to her emotions that even as I gave her pleasure, I received even greater pleasure.

Now I kissed her. Deeply. Passionately. Leisurely. Yet hungrily. Myriad sensations pulsed through me, but the one that inspired all of my movements emanated from the general area of my chest, not my erection. This was new to me, this power center. It was a place I'd never tapped into. Yet one that I never wanted to lose touch with again.

So this was what it meant to make love. I smiled even as we kissed. And we hadn't even had intercourse yet.

While undressing her, I'd placed a handful of condoms on the nightstand, next to her bottles of lotion. I reached for a packet now, taking my time as I sheathed myself. I'd taken an unnecessary risk before without thought to her wants and needs. But not now. Now I understood what it meant to put another person before yourself. What Molly thought, how she felt, was all-important to me.

"I love you."

The words could have easily come from my own mouth, given my train of thought. But they hadn't. Instead Molly had whispered them. And appeared shocked to have done so.

She began to avert her gaze. I gently held her head still in my hands. "Don't," I murmured, kissing her again. "Don't turn away from it, Molly. Please." I briefly closed my eyes, savoring what the spontaneous expression of her feelings meant. I pulled back again to look at her. "I've spent so much of my life running away from things. Feeling like I've been pressed into one role or another. Like I wasn't the one in control but was being controlled. By fate, by life, by love."

She quietly watched me, not saying anything even as her eyes said it all.

"It's only now, when I've finally willingly given up that control—given up my heart—to you that I realize how stupid I've been. I was so busy fighting that I never took the time to stop and see how beautiful it all is. And maybe that's what I've been afraid of all along. I mean, when you reach the point where you have everything you ever need in life…what else is there?"

I heard her swallow. "And the answer?"

I positioned myself again between her thighs. "This."

I slowly sank into her silken flesh to the hilt, each precious inch filling me to overflowing with emotion and heat, elevating my heartbeat, causing the golden cloud in my chest to expand until it completely enveloped me…enveloped us.

Us.

I began to slowly withdraw, incapable of faster movement as I stroked her, my only goal to move her soul. We were no longer separate travelers on the way to a common destination but joined together.

I couldn't be sure how long we made love. It could have been twenty minutes. It could have been two hours. But as our bodies demonstrated what our hearts felt, we climbed to a place unfamiliar to me. And breath-stealing-ly exquisite.

And I couldn't think of another person on earth I'd rather be there with.

As the first waves of crises crashed against my insides, I kissed her lingeringly. "And I love you, Molly Laraway."

# 18

MOLLY CRACKED HER EYES open, not wanting the dream to end. Alan's arms tightened around her, pulling her backside flush against his front. She smiled and snuggled closer still, realizing it wasn't a dream but delicious reality.

On the bedside table lay the remnants of the breakfast they'd fed each other around dawn. It had been more for fortification than to satisfy any real desire for food. But that hadn't meant they couldn't find new and inventive ways to feed each other strawberries and cream. Her body was sticky for myriad reasons, and her pillow was smeared with chocolate, but she couldn't bring herself to move more than what it took to get closer to Alan.

She became aware of something tugging at her hair. Rather he seemed to be stroking the strands. Maybe to get some sort of food or other out of it.

"I don't think I've ever done this," he said quietly.

She shifted until she was lying on her other side, facing him. "Done what?"

Stubble shadowed his jawline once again. When

combined with his tousled hair, it gave him a look that went beyond sexy.

"Played hooky from work."

She leaned closer as if to kiss his mouth but instead kissed his chin. "Well, then, I think it's long past time that you did."

He chuckled and held her head against his chest, where she'd moved her attention. "I do, too."

Molly remembered the only time she'd played hooky. It had been with her sister, the day before final exams their senior year. Claire had convinced her to skip, saying she needed help cramming for the intensive tests, that she was afraid that without Molly's help she would fail.

The thought of accepting her diploma without her sister by her side as she'd been every step of her life had hit her like a fist to the chest. So she'd agreed.

And she and her sister had done everything but study until much later that night.

"Where did you go?" Alan asked when she'd shared the story.

Molly pressed her nose against his chest and kissed him. "A golf course."

"You went golfing?"

"No, I said we went to a golf course. We didn't play. We'd gone walking through a public parkway and spotted the course through the trees. So there we lay on the eighth green, staring at the clouds and talking about…I don't know. Everything. Our futures. Our dreams."

"Don't tell me. You wanted to be Ally McBeal."

She lightly bit into the soft flesh of his chest and he feigned pain. "At that point, no. I mean, I knew I wanted to go into law, but I didn't know in what capacity. It wasn't until later that I decided to be an attorney."

"And your sister?"

"Wanted to be Miss America."

Molly smiled at the memory, remembering the way she'd rolled her eyes. And how her sister had looked hurt. She hadn't realized how serious Claire had been until that moment. Until after she'd thoughtlessly stomped all over her sister's dream.

"Hey," Alan said, making her realize she'd fallen silent. "You okay?"

He tipped her head back and looked into her face.

"Yeah," she said. "I'm okay. But Claire never will be again."

Molly snuggled closer to his chest and lay there. Just lay there. Allowing everything that had happened over the past few weeks to flow over her. Had anyone told her that her life would have changed so drastically within such a short time span, she'd have scoffed.

And if it was true that when one door closed, a window opened, then she had the very distinct impression that Alan was on the other side of that window.

A chirp of a cell phone.

Alan groaned. "Don't answer it."

"It's not mine," she said, not recognizing the ringtone.

"Shit."

She held him tighter. "Don't answer it."

"Unfortunately I have to," he said. "Like a doctor, I'm always on call. Only my job comes *after* a person dies."

Molly gave him the room he needed to reach for his phone, then she snuggled back into the cradle of his arms, loving the way he stroked her bare back.

"Chevalier."

Molly made out the tinny sound of a woman's voice.

"Have someone else look into it."

He moved his hand a little farther south, cupping her bottom. Molly gave a wiggle and shifted so that he had easy access to other nearby areas.

"What do you mean I'd be the one who'd want to check this out?"

His hand froze.

"I'll be right there."

Molly moved away at the same time as he rolled the other way and straight out of bed. She pulled the sheet up to her chest.

"What is it?" she hardly dared ask.

He jerked on his boxers, then his pants, his face registering shock. "There's been another Quarter killing."

Fear iced Molly's spine as she snapped upright.

"Apparently the victim is my ex-wife."

THUD-THUD. THUD-THUD. The constant sound of my heartbeat was about all I was capable of concentrating on as I stood in the doorway of Valerie's bedroom. There she lay, her head hanging over the edge of her bed, her throat slit, her eyes seeming to stare at me in some eerie postmortem greeting. I imagined her saying, "Hey, Alan. How are you doing? Me? Not so well."

I turned from the scene, for the first time in a very long time feeling like I might be sick.

"Hey, you all right?" Steven asked me, having arrived on the scene before me and already setting to work.

"What the hell do you think?"

Jackson held his hands up. "Don't unload on me. I'm the one who didn't think it was a good idea you be contacted yet."

Val had kept her married name, so it would have taken very little checking to find out she was my ex-wife.

Christ. I stalked from the small house, started walking up the street, then traced a path back again, seeking clarity in a situation that made no sense.

Val....

Had it really only been three days ago she'd insisted I meet her for lunch so she could tell me what a sloppy, irresponsible drunk I was becoming? Demand that I seek help for my sisters' sake? For my own sake?

I began pacing again, unable to find purchase on

the situation. Val, who took great pride in taking care of everyone but herself. Val, who was now lying dead inside the house she'd moved into after our split. Val, who would still be alive had I been doing my job right and found the goddamn Quarter Killer before he struck again.

I walked to the corner and leaned against the brick wall of a closed restaurant, curiously out of breath, my mind spinning.

Sweet Jesus. Val was dead.

# 19

LATER IN THE DAY, MOLLY returned to her hotel room. She'd left the Do Not Disturb sign on the door when she'd left earlier, yet she discovered that maid service had called anyway, cleaning away all traces of Alan's having been there the night before.

She stripped the spread from the bed with an unsettled yank, then sank to the mattress, wishing that she had a pillow that smelled of him to hold close to her chest.

Wishing even more that she could reach him.

As she lay back across the bed, the rational side of her argued that he had a job to do. Doubly so now that the latest victim was tied to him personally. But all she could think about was how devastated she'd been when she'd gotten the call about Claire. She'd needed someone to turn to, but there had been no one. Certainly not her mother, who had not only seemed unsurprised by the news of her daughter's death but seemed almost to have expected it.

Of course, Molly knew now that was the way her mother dealt with tragedy. You turned your head the other way, pretended you knew what was coming all along and kept on walking until you didn't feel anything anymore.

And that was what Molly had done for the better part of today. She'd walked. While she hadn't been able to turn away emotionally from the impact of everything that had happened lately, she had been successful in physically exhausting herself. Her feet and legs ached, at least matching the pain in her chest at the thought of Alan out there dealing with the death of his ex-wife alone.

She pulled a pillow to her chest anyway, imagining she could smell him. Only he wasn't really alone, was he? He had his sisters. And it was that thought that had brought her some comfort. And had also inspired her to look into his third sister's absence on her own. While she held out little hope that she'd be successful in finding Zoe, she knew that now, especially today, Alan and the rest of his family didn't need the added worry of their sister's absence.

She only hoped that circumstances were as Alan suspected and that the youngest Chevalier sibling was indeed missing by choice rather than by the hand of another.

Should something have happened to her, as well…

She refused to think about that possibility. Refused to consider what that might do to Alan.

She recalled seeing him yesterday at the Gas Lantern. How different he'd looked. The way he'd refused the bourbon. And how she'd sensed—and later verified—that he'd undergone some very important changes. How would those changes be affected by the death of his ex? By news of something bad having befallen Zoe?

She forced herself off the bed and moved to stand at the large window, staring at the historic French Quarter below. Dusk was just beginning to fall and lights were being turned on. Tourists and locals alike walked the narrow streets, some in costume, others not. She wondered where Alan was right that minute.

And wondered if they'd ever be able to make their way back to where they'd been that morning while they'd lain in bed together.

I WAS WORKING ON AUTOPILOT. After a day spent in a blur questioning Val's neighbors and friends and coworkers, I'd had to face the fact that I needed to tell my sisters about my ex-wife's death before they found out via an outside source. I couldn't stand the thought of them hearing about it that way. So at just after noon I'd headed uptown to the old house in the Garden District. Emilie had been home alone, feeding lunch to a fussy Henri. I'd asked her to call Laure and have her come from work, unable to face the task of telling them both separately. I hadn't considered that they'd both think the news I had to share involved Zoe. So I'd been a little surprised by their immediate looks of relief, followed quickly by grief at the death of someone they'd come to see as an important member of the family, the closest thing to a mother they'd had since the loss of their stepmother.

I'd stayed as long as I could. But I couldn't be around the tears without wanting to succumb to some of my own. So I'd left them with the task of contacting Val's family members and seeing to funeral plans.

Funeral plans.

Christ.

Now, long after the sun had set, the smell of stale pizza filling the room, I sat at my desk, going through the pile of paperwork there, searching for something—anything—that would help me find the bastard who had done this and nail him to the wall by his balls.

"I didn't find anything in here," John said, placing on the corner of my desk a neat pile of files I'd given him to go through.

"Look again," I said without glancing up.

He checked his watch. "Do you have any idea what time it is?"

Time was no longer of importance to me. All that mattered was finding the person responsible for killing Molly's sister and my ex-wife.

As I thought it, I moved a forensics report, and the picture Molly had given me during our first lunch stared up at me. I picked it up, looking down at the two college grads beaming into the camera lens. I remembered her story of how they had played hooky on a golf course only a short time before then. I rubbed my eyes.

"It's just after two in the morning," John said.

I blinked at that. If pressed to guess, I would have said somewhere around nine.

"Whatever might be in any of this can wait a couple of hours."

I snapped my gaze to his tired face. "Wait for what, Roche? For the killer to strike again? What, if anything, do you know about serial killers?"

John looked ready to fall over with exhaustion. He sat down instead and pulled the folders back into his lap. "That the time between killings shortens after each incident."

"So there were three weeks between the time of Claire Laraway's murder and Val's. Which means…"

"Which means odds are the time span will be significantly less between now and the next murder."

I slapped the report in my hands to the desk. "So get back to work."

I opened a desk drawer, the familiar clinking of a bottle inside catching my attention as John wandered back to his desk on the other side of the quiet room. I sat staring down at the bourbon, swallowing the saliva that flooded my mouth at the sight of it. Just one drink. What would it hurt? It would take the edge off and help me think.

I slammed the drawer shut against the bourbon

and my weak thoughts, clenching my jaw. No, liquor would only dull my senses. Slow me up.

But one thing would help me. Rather one person. Molly.

I grabbed my coat and my hat and made for the door. Stopping just inside, I said over my shoulder, "You're right, Roche. We're both operating on fumes now. Go home. Get some rest. But I want to see you back in here on the ass of dawn, got it?"

"Got it."

THE FOLLOWING MORNING Molly had what she'd longed for: the scent of Alan on her pillow. But rather than bringing her peace, it was a source for sadness. Because while Alan had been there physically, he hadn't been there emotionally.

She felt a sob well up in her throat and fought it back. There had been no soft caresses, no lingering kisses. Even when she'd cuddled up alongside him, he'd seemed cold, detached. As if all the walls that had come tumbling down over the past few days had been built back up, but this time with material she couldn't hope to break through or scale.

As she lay there alone now watching the morning sun climb in the sky outside her hotel room window, she felt used. As if she'd been only a means to an end for him. A replacement for the bourbon he'd cast aside.

When she'd awakened earlier this morning, alone,

no note in his wake, she'd barely remembered how relieved she'd been when he'd knocked at her door at two-thirty. And how surprised she'd been by his voiceless, passionless demand for sex.

She'd tried to inject warmth into their kisses, but every time, he'd pulled away from her and focused on a body part. Making what should have been more intimate instead more alienating.

There was a knock at the door.

Molly lifted her head to look at the clock. Just after nine.

Alan?

She wasn't sure if her heart clenched in hope or pain.

Then again, it was probably maid service.

She squeezed her eyes shut. Yesterday they'd asked if she still planned to leave. When she'd originally checked in, she'd told them she'd be staying a week and would let them know if she needed the room for longer. Only she'd forgotten to extend the checkout date, and now they already had her room booked, revelers coming into town for Halloween quickly snatching it up.

So now she had to find another hotel.

"I'll be checking out at noon," she shouted.

"Ma'am, I have a delivery here for you."

Delivery?

She finally climbed from the too-large bed, pulled on the white hotel robe, then opened the door.

A hotel clerk stood holding a package stamped with an overnight-delivery sticker.

Claire's lockbox.

THE FACE I SAW IN THE lab mirror was familiar to me. A lot more familiar than the clean-shaven one I'd glimpsed a couple of days ago. And the inside of me reflected the outside. While I still hadn't had a drink, lack of sleep and plenty of self-loathing made me feel like I'd done considerable damage to a fifth last night.

The problem was, the only one I'd done damage to was Molly.

I winced and turned away from the mirror.

Near dawn I could have sworn I'd heard her crying. Only she was deep asleep. Rather than wake her and try to comfort her, I'd climbed from the bed and left her lying there alone.

This morning had been the first time I'd had a chance to stop and think about anything but the case. And it had occurred to me to put out an APB on my little sister, Zoe—something I'd done first thing.

Steven came in from a room off the main one carrying a tray of test tubes.

"It's about damn time, Chan. I've been waiting here for a half hour."

"You've been waiting five minutes," he said, appearing my exact opposite, looking rested and alert in his cleanly pressed lab coat.

He sat down at a table filled with instruments, and I moved to stand alongside him.

"What do you got for me?"

"Definitely the same killer as in the Laraway case." He opened a file and made an additional notation before handing it to me. "It appears the same knife was used, particles a perfect match. Same MO, except in the Chevalier case—" he slanted me a look "—in the *second* case, there's no sign of intercourse." He lifted a finger. "However, interestingly enough, there were traces of semen in the victim's vagina."

I stared at him. "How can there be a presence of sperm with no penetration?"

"Premature ejaculation maybe?"

"Jesus." I didn't really want to be discussing items of this nature about my ex. Especially since I had information that not even Jackson did. That Val had taken a gay lover about a year ago and during lunch the other day she'd indicated they were still going strong. Another woman, incapable of producing sperm.

"There was also a hair placed in this victim's wound, as well. Perfect match to the hair found in the first victim's."

"Like it was purposely placed there."

"Right. Root and all."

I stared at him. "So where does that leave us?"

"It leaves us with two victims murdered by the same killer."

"No additional evidence? No footprints found on

the scene? Trace evidence not linked to the first crime? Fingerprints?"

"Oh. Interesting you should mention that."

I perked up. "You got something."

"Not in the way you think." He stood, walked to a filing cabinet, then took out a bag that held a familiar item: Claire Laraway's diary.

"Don't tell me you've been wasting your time on that."

Steven smiled at me. "At the time, I didn't have anything else to do. I was going to call you with the information first thing yesterday morning, but I got sidetracked."

By Val's murder. He didn't have to say it.

"Anyway," he said, "I found several sets of prints on the journal and ran them through the computer."

"And?"

"And you'll never believe what I came up with."

If all this was leading to some sort of joke, I was going to coldcock him.

"See here," he said, obviously enjoying drawing this out. "I lifted a partial thumbprint from the upper left-hand corner of the cover."

I kept staring at him instead of looking at the diary.

"You know how all homicide and forensics personnel, past and present, have their prints on file for elimination purposes? Well, this print belongs to none other than your dear friend and mine, Captain Seymour Hodge."

# 20

MOLLY PACED THE WALKWAY in front of the coffee shop, waiting for Claude Lafitte. Immediately upon receiving the lockbox, she'd called Akela to get access to the key Molly had given her. Unfortunately the FBI agent was in Quantico for some sort of daylong seminar, but she'd arranged to have Claude bring Molly the key at the coffee shop.

She looked at her watch. He was already ten minutes late.

She turned to pace the other way and spotted him walking in her direction. "Thank God. I thought you'd gotten held up somewhere."

"Sorry I'm late," he said in that rumbling voice of his. "Do you want to go in here?"

She nodded and he opened the door for her. She grabbed the first table she came to, although Claude was eyeing a table at the back.

"This shouldn't take long," she said. "Do you have the key?"

He produced it from his front pocket. Once she'd

accepted it, she briefly closed her eyes and said a silent prayer before trying it in the lock.

It fit perfectly.

The lid sprang up to reveal a series of photographs and some money.

Molly looked up at Claude. He shrugged.

After pushing a series of hundred-dollar bills aside, she picked up the photos. Claude moved closer to her to see them, as well.

They all seemed to have been taken on the same day, judging by the purple blouse Claire wore. Molly's heart gave a gentle squeeze, recognizing it as her sister's favorite. In the pictures with her was a man. Older. Molly flipped to the next one. At least it appeared so. She couldn't really tell because in each of the pictures he was blocking a full-on shot in some way. Either he'd lifted an arm or had turned away, and in one he'd lifted a pillow to hide behind.

Claire's married man, "C"? It seemed likely.

"Do you recognize him?" Molly asked Claude.

He shook his head. "*Non.* Not that there's much to recognize. Obviously the man was determined not to have his picture taken."

And just as obviously Claire had seemed determined to take it.

Claude took the photos and leafed through them. Then he handed them back to her.

"Nothing."

Molly looked through them more slowly, this time

focusing on her sister. Her sister was obviously the one holding the camera. Sometimes fully behind it, other times holding it out to snap a shot of the couple together.

Claire had never looked happier.

Molly swallowed thickly.

"You okay, *chère?*"

Molly nodded, placed the photos in the box, then closed it again, thinking it not a good idea to count the cash in public. "I guess I'll keep the key, then." Claude got up and waited for her to do the same. They exited the coffee shop without ordering anything. "Tell Akela I'll bring the box by when she gets back."

"That would be tomorrow."

"Very well, then." She forced a smile, trying to hide her disappointment that the box hadn't held something more definitive. "Thanks, Claude."

"Don't mention it."

I'D LEARNED LONG AGO that there was no such thing as coincidence. Hodge's print was on that diary; he was connected to the murder.

"Detective Chevalier! Wait! You can't just walk in there!"

I'd also learned that the surest way past a secretary was never to stop.

I opened the door to Captain Hodge's office, then closed it after myself. He looked up from where he was sitting at his desk, talking on the phone.

I crossed the room and tossed the bag with the

diary in it on his desktop. "What in the hell are your fingerprints doing all over this?"

His eyes narrowed. "Honey, I've got to go. No, I'm not trying to get rid of you." Seymour glared at me, then turned his chair away. "I promise. Something urgent just came up. Yes, sweetcakes, I'll call you back the minute I'm done."

Listening to him talk to Astrid robbed a bit of the wind from my sails. But not much.

"What in the hell do you mean barging in like this, Chevalier?" he asked, getting up from his chair.

There weren't very many men who intimated me. But Seymour Hodge was one of them. It was more than just his height and hefty build. There was something dangerous about him. It's what had made him a top homicide detective when he was younger. And what made him an effective captain now.

It was also what landed him the number one spot on my previously nonexistent list of suspects.

"What are your fingerprints doing on this?" I held up the diary.

He crossed his arms over his chest and stared at the object. "I'm sure I don't know. What is it?"

"It's an item belonging to the Quarter Killer's first victim."

He narrowed his gaze. "That's impossible."

"No, it's reality. What I want to know is how in the hell one of your prints got there."

He rounded his desk and came to stand in front of

me. "You aren't actually accusing me of a crime, are you, Detective Chevalier?"

"I'm accusing you of having touched an item of evidence that the chain of custody never puts in your immediate vicinity."

He took the bag, looked at the diary through it, then handed it back to me. "Is this part of the victim's personal belongings that Agent Brooks was in possession of?"

I didn't answer.

"Because if it is, I believe she brought a box of such items by here when she was trying to prove her lover innocent."

I snatched the bag from his hand, then pointed at him. "If you had anything—and I mean anything—to do with this, Seymour, I swear on my father's grave that I'll nail your sorry ass to the wall behind you. Do you hear me?"

"Fair enough. And when you discover that I have absolutely no connection to the murders, I'm going to enjoy firing your sorry ass. Do I make myself clear?"

I resisted the urge to sucker punch him right then and there.

Instead I turned and stormed from the room, nearly knocking his secretary over where she'd been listening on the other side of the door.

MOLLY STOOD OUTSIDE the seedy motel room at the end of a row of others and stared at the address Thor had given her. Left with nothing much to occupy her time aside from worrying about Alan and, well, feeling sorry for herself, she'd decided to do some checking around on Alan's sister Zoe. She hadn't really expected anything to come from her return visit to the Goth bar on Bourbon Street, but she'd been surprised to find that Thor and the girl with the purple streaks had not only been there but they had been friendlier yet, embracing her as a friend despite her change in apparel to jeans and a plain black top. Maybe because she'd been wearing black.

"Yeah, I know Fawn," Thor had said.

She'd stared at him. "Well, why didn't you say anything last time I was here?"

He'd shrugged and grinned. "Because you didn't ask."

A half hour—and a half an iridescent red drink later—she'd been armed with the address to the motel room she now stood outside of.

And wondering just what in the hell she thought she was doing.

Molly stuffed the paper bearing the address into her front pocket, trying to decide if she should knock on the door or leave. Zoe didn't know her from Adam. And she wasn't sure how the twenty-one-year-old would view her meddling in matters that were really none of her concern.

Maybe she should just give the information to Alan. Or, better yet, to one of his other sisters.

Instead she found herself knocking on the motel-room door, her palms damp, her resolve slipping with each second she waited for someone to answer.

Nobody there.

She began to turn around when a lock turned and the door opened inward to reveal the young woman from Alan's picture, wearing nothing but a towel… and a wedding ring.

"ROUGH DAY, C?"

I scowled at where Jack Cadieux took a seat across from me at the Gas Lantern. While he did that every now and again, tonight…well, tonight I would just as soon be alone.

*Oh, yeah? If that's the case, then why aren't you at home?*

Because drinking at a booze can didn't make you feel as guilty as when you did it alone at home.

"You could say that," I mumbled, a piss-poor attempt at civility.

"Your lady friend coming tonight?"

I squinted at him. He had to mean Molly. And while somewhere in the back of my bourbon-addled brain I secretly hoped that she would stop by, my gut told me she wouldn't.

Not that I blamed her. I'd treated her like crap the last time I'd seen her. Something I seemed to be doing a lot of.

"What's all this? Bringing work home with you?"

Jack gestured to the files littering the top of the table, which I'd scoured for the umpteenth time, looking for something—anything—that would give me a lead on the killer.

But it was Jack using the word *home* in conjunction with the bar that bothered me. Partly because he was right. Mostly because I was coming to realize that home didn't lie in a house or an apartment but with a person. In my case, a person I couldn't allow myself to have.

"Yeah, something like that," I said.

He held up his hands. "Hey, you don't have to hit me over the head. I can take a hint that you don't want company."

I watched as he got up and walked back to the bar.

The place was quiet tonight, most of the Halloween revelers choosing to party in the Quarter proper, where most of the action was. Which was just fine with me. I reached for the half-empty bottle, stared at it, then poured a healthy portion into my empty glass as an empty sign of defiance.

Hell, I was going down anyway. Why not go down in a haze of glory?

I rubbed my numb face, thinking of my meeting with Hodge earlier. Meeting. Now there was a word for you. What I'd done hadn't been anything less than stupid. Whereas I might have gained a bit of sympathy, seeing as my ex-wife had fallen victim to the Quarter Killer, I'd burned it all and then some by accusing Hodge of having a connection to Claire Laraway.

And I hadn't even been drinking.

"You're fucking lucky he didn't fire you on the spot," I said aloud, pushing the glass aside and reaching instead for the file in front of me.

I pored over the report on the first victim, trying to push out of my mind the fact that it was Molly's sister. I turned over the postmortem photo of her so I could focus on the report instead.

Semen found not matching the DNA of suspect.

Of course, the DNA report had come after. And since Claude Lafitte was a consummate ladies' man who probably owned stock in a prophylactic company, it had been a pretty good guess that the semen had come from the killer.

I leafed through another file until I came up with the still shot taken from the security camera across from Hotel Josephine. It had been blown up and was too grainy to make out anything more than a darkly clothed figure wearing a head scarf and big, dark sunglasses. A woman? That was what we'd all believed. But if the suspect was a woman, where had the semen come from?

Jackson had theorized that Claire Laraway may have had another sexual conquest right before she'd met Claude Lafitte. But her friends had sworn a statement saying she'd been with them for at least four hours before she'd met up with Lafitte and liaised with him at the hotel.

I looked back at the original file.

Traces of K-Y jelly had been found mixed with the semen.

But Claire had been on the pill, and no tube of the stuff had been found in any of her things.

Then there was the fact that semen had been found in Val's body, although there had been no sign of sex.

I realized I was crumpling the report in my fist. I let it go and tried to smooth it out.

It was here, damn it. I knew it was. Hiding somewhere in the maze of forensics reports and witness interviews was the map to the killer.

My cell phone vibrated in my pocket. I absently reached for it, not taking the time to look at the display because I'd taken so long to answer.

"Chevalier."

"Alan? It's Laure."

I sat up straight, as if trying to appear sober even though she couldn't see me through the phone.

"Zoe's home."

# 21

MOLLY SAT IN THE HOTEL coffee shop, staring out at the street beyond. She'd had a difficult time obtaining a reservation at any of the hotels she'd prefer to stay in and had only lucked out when someone had called to cancel their reservation. People milled everywhere inside and outside the unfamiliar hotel. She glanced at her watch. It was after midnight. Officially All Hallow's Eve.

She wrapped her arms around herself to fend off a shiver.

There was so much about this city that was foreign to her. In Toledo, the fall colors would be in full swing, reds and yellows and oranges setting the green landscape on fire. Temperatures would be cool, sweaters and jackets a must, and on some nights a parka required. Nights out would include a visit to the cinema or a bookstore or a local bar to catch a classic-rock cover band.

She slowly sipped her herb tea, the sound of jazz inescapable, even being piped through the coffee shop. Where people rushed around up north, here life moved at a slower pace. She, too, didn't feel the need to be doing something every second of every day. Life wasn't something to catch up with but rather something to savor.

Of course, she also recognized that much of her new mind-set had to do with the circumstances surrounding her. Losing Claire. Hunting for the killer. Letting Alan—and now, by extension, his family—into her life.

She sat back in her chair. No doubt Zoe was at the big house Alan had told her about, with her sisters and even possibly her brother, her new husband in tow.

And Molly? While she felt a part of the picture, she really wasn't. She was a temporary visitor from a place so outside New Orleans as to be a foreign country. Even her mother had failed to ask when she might be coming home when Molly had called to tell her of the nearly five thousand dollars in cash that had been in the lockbox. She'd promised to wire the money—minus the cost of sending it—to her mother first thing in the morning. Although by all rights she should have kept it to go toward the expense of Claire's funeral arrangements. Arrangements she'd seen to and paid for.

She abruptly got up from the chair, unable to sit for another moment, wallowing in self-pity. While the city might encourage a more relaxed approach to life, she'd never been one to sit back and allow things to happen. She needed to be involved.

And part of that involvement included finding her

sister's killer so she could get back to her own life, in a place far, far from here.

She gathered her purse, put a tip on the table, then headed out the main lobby doors, where even at this late hour a line of taxis waited. She hailed one and gave him a familiar address. She only hoped Alan would be home.

"WHAT DO YOU MEAN YOU got married?" I demanded of a red-eyed Zoe at the Chevalier house.

After Laure's phone call, I'd asked Jack to ply me with coffee—and lots of it—along with water, my desire to sober up as quickly as possible a top priority. Damn my weakness.

Now here I was, facing off with my baby sister, wanting to hug her and throttle her simultaneously.

"Do you have any idea how worried I was? How worried we all were? There's a killer on the loose, and you choose to run off to Mexico to elope with a guy we've never met without letting anyone know?"

I watched as with each word Zoe sank deeper and deeper into the sofa, her knees pulled to her chest.

It amazed me how quickly she could turn into that little girl being scolded for bringing a stray dog home and allowing it to destroy nearly everything on the first floor. Thankfully I'd gotten home in time to stop the mutt from finding the second floor.

Of course, I'd allowed Zoe to keep the hound from hell. In the fenced-in backyard.

"There's always a killer on the loose here," she said in a small voice.

Christ. The kid was only two months over the legal drinking age. And now she was married? What was she thinking?

I glanced into the other room at her husband, who looked at least as young as she was and inspired a desire in me to drag him out back and wreak havoc on his face. I was pretty sure I growled.

I turned back to Zoe.

"Alan, please," Emilie said, taking my arm and urging me into the dining room with her.

I went, but not willingly.

"She feels bad enough for what she did already. Don't make this worse than it is."

I knew she was talking about Zoe's learning of Val's death. Of the three girls, Zoe had been the most attached to my ex. Probably because she'd been so young—eleven—when our parents had died.

Emilie sighed heavily, apparently having a hard time dealing with everything herself. "I'm just thankful that your friend Molly brought her back to us."

I'd been glaring at Zoe's sorry excuse for a husband—more boyfriend material than husband—and now snapped my gaze back to Emilie so fast I thought I heard something snap in my neck. "What?"

Emilie blinked at me. "You didn't know? It's the first thing Zoe said. That some woman named Molly, a friend of yours, came knocking at the door of the motel room she and Matthew were staying at and told her she should get in contact with us as soon as possible. That there's been a family emergency."

Molly....

I turned from Emilie to Zoe, where she was now openly watching me from the other room. Molly had found his sister? But how? And why?

"Oh, and she gave something to Zoe to give to you. Let me go get it."

I stalked into the living room again, considered Zoe long and hard, then asked, "Are you pregnant?"

"Pregnant? God, that's just like you." She rolled her red eyes. "I use protection, Alan."

Well, at least she had the good sense to do that much. "The pill?"

"No, a diaphragm. My body doesn't react well to the hormones in the pill."

Diaphragm....

My mind clicked on an image, then backtracked, following a path of bread crumbs.

Shit.

I stalked toward the door, then stopped and made my way back to the couch where Zoe sat. I leaned over and cupped the back of her head with my hand, briefly marveling at the softness, then kissed her forehead.

"I'm glad you're okay, kid."

I moved toward the door again.

"Hold on," Emilie said, hurrying into the room.

She held out what looked like a photograph. "This is what Molly left for Zoe to give to you."

I stared down at the picture of Claire with a man I clearly recognized, even with the arm in front of his face.

The elusive "C" hadn't been an initial for a man with a name beginning with the letter. Rather Claire had used it as a shortened version for Seymour.

More specifically, Captain Seymour Hodge.

Jackpot.

I strode purposefully toward the door.

"What about the funeral arrangements?" Emilie asked, hugging herself with her arms.

"They can wait until tomorrow."

Everything could wait, period. Because dread spread through my bloodstream like a cold drug. If things were as I thought they were, chances were Molly was in danger.

MOLLY STOOD ON THE street outside Alan's apartment, watching as the taxi drove off. She'd thought of asking the driver to stay in case Alan wasn't home, then decided that if he wasn't there, he would have to come back at some point. She would wait. There were too many unsaid things that needed to be stated. And the sooner the better.

She looked at the apartment above. It was dark. Which didn't bode well for her chances of his being home. She was able to turn to look for his car, but as she watched, a light switched on in his apartment. The kitchen? It appeared so.

The wind picked up, blowing her hair across her face and giving her the first sense since she'd been down here that it was autumn. A few leaves traveled on the air, somersaulting down the street.

She shivered and forced herself to go to the front door of the building, then up the stairs, until she stood in front of Alan's apartment door. A jumble of emotions swirled through her. This was a man who had touched her in a way no other had before him. Made her feel special, loved, cherished. Then just as easily turned his back on her and made her feel used.

She'd known from the beginning that demons battled within him. Dark, demanding ghosts that he chased away with bourbon when he returned home alone at night. But while she'd come to learn a bit about what had brought the unwanted visitors into his life, she couldn't begin to fathom what it was like to be inside his mind, to live in his heart.

The only thing she knew was that she wanted to try.

No, *had* to try.

*Molly, do you believe that out there somewhere is that one person meant especially for you?*

She heard Claire's question as clearly as if her sister stood in front of her asking it.

*You mean, like a soul mate?*

*Yes.*

Her twin had posed the question during a phone

conversation shortly after she'd moved to New Orleans. Molly had been at work, poring over legal tomes for a precedent to help prove a case she was working on. She'd had a headache the size of Ohio and hadn't realized it was well after five until Claire had called.

*No,* she'd said.

Claire had laughed. *I knew you'd say that.*

Then she'd fallen silent.

Molly had thought about ringing off with the excuse that she had work to do and didn't have time to indulge in such wistful talk. But something had kept her on the line.

Maybe hope that what Claire had to say next might convince her she was wrong.

*I didn't think I believed, either. Not until today, anyway.*

Had that been the day her sister had met her married lover? The man she'd called *C* in her diary? The man who was possibly her killer?

*Remember all those times when Mom said she was searching for the man who would complete her?*

Molly remembered. She also remembered that their mother's hunt had ended up with her and Claire calling dozens of strange men "Uncle."

*Well, I think maybe that's why I never believed. Because if Mom couldn't find what she was looking for—and she'd been looking so hard—I thought that it couldn't possibly be true.*

Molly's heart had hurt at that. She hadn't realized until that moment how damaged she and her sister had been by their mother's activities. Had they both turned their heads away from love because they'd been convinced it didn't exist?

*But it is true,* Claire had whispered. *Oh, Molly, it is.*

And Molly had known that at that moment in time for Claire, it was true.

And now…now she knew it to be the truth, herself. Because no matter how challenging he was, and how much he had the capacity to bring her pain, the man who completed her was broken, wounded, demon-filled Alan. He was the dark to her light. He'd brought life into the empty void of her existence. He'd made her see things she hadn't known existed. And no matter how much she tried to convince herself that she could go back to the way things were before she'd met him, she knew that was impossible. She'd been irrevocably changed.

What remained was what she decided to do about it.

She blinked the door to Alan's apartment back into view, reaching out a hand to touch the wood rather than to knock. It creaked open under her fingers. The scent of a woman's perfume, expensive and overpowering, assaulted her nose. But she couldn't be sure if it was coming from inside the apartment or down the hall.

"Alan?" she called softly.

She craned her neck to see into the darkness. If she'd seen light from the street, there was no evidence of it now. Had he gone to bed? Or was he sitting inside in the dark?

She pushed the door farther inward, repeating his name.

It took a moment for her eyes to adjust. When blackness turned into shades of gray and outlines of furniture, she reached back and closed the door after herself.

And the minute she heard the lock click home, she felt a blow to the back of her head that plunged her into an unyielding darkness.

# 22

"WHAT DO YOU MEAN SHE'S checked out?"

It was all I could do not to grab the tie the guy at the Ritz's front desk wore and use it as a garrote.

"I'm sorry, Detective, but that's what it says here. She checked out yesterday at noon."

I looked down at the computer screen he was consulting as if I could make heads or tails out of what he was reading. "Does it give a forwarding address?"

"Let me look…."

I paced a short ways away, reaching for my hat, only to realize I must have left it at my sisters' house. Damn. I ran my fingers through my hair instead.

"No, I'm sorry, sir, there's no forwarding address listed."

I stormed from the lobby, taking in everything and everyone around me. Why would Molly check out? Obviously she was still in town, because she'd succeeded in finding my youngest sister.

Or maybe the gesture had been her last before she'd finally given up on finding her own sister's killer and headed back home to Toledo.

My heart thundered in my chest at not knowing where she was. Whether she was safe. What she was doing.

The tires squealed as I pulled away from the curb, heading to…I didn't know where.

MOLLY WAS HAVING THE dream again. The one where she was Claire on the morning she'd been murdered. She felt the cold blade of a knife being pressed against her throat. The warmth of her own blood seeping out of her wound, dripping onto the sheets of the bed she lay on.

Gasping for air, she snapped upright—only to find a weight on her hips preventing her from moving.

"Stay still, you little whore."

A woman's voice. And if her nose was correct, she was the source of the stifling perfume Molly had smelled at the entrance of Alan's apartment.

Alan.

"I don't understand," the woman said, ripping the front of Molly's shirt open. "I already killed you. I already killed you. How could you have survived? I already killed you."

Molly's lungs refused air as she fought to hold her destroyed shirt together. The woman's words left little doubt in her mind as to their meaning: she was her sister's murderer.

And she thought Molly was Claire.

Her captor straddled her hips, effectively pinning

her to the bed. Molly's legs felt like deadweight and her head pounded where she'd taken the hit. How long had she been out of it? And what was the woman doing in Alan's apartment?

She frantically looked around the apartment from her vantage point but could make out little in the darkness.

"Please," she said. "I'm not Claire."

Her captor caught her around the throat. In the dimness Molly could see that she wore all black. And that she was a complete stranger to her.

"Don't you lie to me, slut! What do you take me for, an idiot? I'll never forget your face. Not when you came to my house with your little story, ruining my life by telling me my husband loved you. You!" Her fingers tightened and Molly coughed in reflex. "I paid you to stay away from him. You took the goddamn money and kept seeing him anyway." Her voice grew shriller. "Did you think I wouldn't find out? Did you think I was stupid? Well, Astrid Devereaux Hodge might be a lot of things, but stupid is not one of them, do you hear me?"

The name rang a bell somewhere in the cottony depths of Molly's mind.

*Please, please let someone hear her. Let someone hear her screams and call the police.*

Then she remembered where she was. Recalled that down here in the Big Easy people were reluctant to call the police. If an incident didn't have an immediate impact on them, the general populace looked the other way, ignored it, letting things happen that perhaps were meant to.

Panic and dread saturated her muscles as Astrid released her grip on Molly's neck. Molly coughed violently. She could smell leather and realized it was because the other woman was wearing gloves.

"No, no...I must stick to my plan. Stick to my plan."

Molly recognized the way Astrid repeated everything twice, almost in a state of delirium. Dealing with a murderous woman was difficult enough. Facing a deranged murderous woman was even worse. There would be no reasoning. No laying out of the facts. No talking her out of what she was about to do.

With a start she realized that her sister had known her killer. Only it hadn't been the man she loved. It had been his wife.

Hot tears welled up in her eyes. Had Claire tried to debate with the insane woman when she'd woken up to find her in the hotel room she'd shared for one night with Claude Lafitte? Claire had been no lightweight. Molly knew that fact from years of sibling rivalry that had sometimes involved physical tussles.

She definitely would have fought.

Astrid ripped off the rest of Molly's shirt, then tugged at the waist of her slacks.

"What...what are you doing?" Molly whispered, forcing herself to be calm, to get a grip on the situation, waiting for the best time to try to make her escape.

"Revealing you for the whore that you are."

Molly's belt pulled free, and Astrid tossed it over the side of the bed where she'd thrown her shirt.

"That's what they should do to women like you. Forget a scarlet letter. You should be made to walk around naked for the whole world to see what a whore you are."

Her voice broke as if she was close to tears.

"Twenty years. Twenty goddamn years I put into that marriage. The perfect wife. I entertained for him. Helped him land his job as captain of the goddamn precinct. I took care of myself for him. Watched what I ate. Exercised. Bought the best makeup and the prettiest clothes. I even gave up my dream of having children because of him. He didn't want them. Said it would ruin my figure." She had her hands to her head, as if she was hearing voices she didn't want to listen to. "Every day I serviced him. Sometimes twice. Do you know how many times that is in twenty years?"

Molly was too occupied with the information Astrid had just given her.

Hodge. That was the name of Alan's immediate superior. The captain of the precinct where he worked.

And Alan had had an affair with the captain's wife….

The woman who'd killed her sister.

Instinct trumped her fear as she grabbed Astrid's arms and tried to twist her from where she sat on top of her.

The other woman shrieked, fighting her with a power that could be fuelled by nothing less than insanity.

With the strength of her legs combined with her hold on Astrid's hands, Molly managed to throw her off balance, then followed through by shoving her off the bed, to the left. As soon as she was free, she rolled to the right, so that they stood staring at each other across the mattress.

"You're helping him, aren't you?" Astrid accused, waving a knife that looked as if it could have gutted an elephant. "Alan's been hiding you from me so you could all get me out of the way."

Molly's gaze was stuck on the knife, which glinted with light shining in from the window behind her.

"You're probably fucking him, too, aren't you? Of course. Because that's what whores like you do."

This whole "whore" bit was starting to wear on Molly's nerves. Her sister may have been a lot of things, but a whore was not one of them. And neither was she.

Even as she knew quick, clear thinking would be the only thing to see her out of the situation alive, she couldn't help the anger that burgeoned inside her. She eyed where Astrid stood between her and the door, then looked around for something to use to protect herself. Surely there was a bottle of bourbon somewhere. To her surprise, she didn't see any.

She stared at a lamp. But rather than pick it up to ward off attack, she switched it on.

Astrid reacted as though the sudden burst of light had blinded her, moving her arm to shield her eyes and gasping.

"I…am…not…Claire," Molly said evenly. She snatched the top sheet from the bed and wrapped it around her right arm. If she held out any hope of disarming Astrid, she'd need the protection, something to ward off the sharp blade of the knife. "I'm her twin sister. But if you're determined to pursue whatever you had in mind, I'll gladly avenge her death."

Astrid seemed to regain her bearings. While she still held her arm up to shield her eyes, she waved the knife she held.

"Liar. If that's the truth, what are you doing here?"

"She's here because she belongs here," a male voice said.

Alan.

Molly's heart skipped a beat in her chest as she spotted him in the open doorway.

"While you, Astrid, most certainly do not."

His presence seemed to catch Astrid off guard.

Why wasn't he drawing his gun? Molly thought in a panic.

He held out his arms. "Christ, Astrid, what are you doing?"

The older woman looked a word away from collapsing in grief. "Oh, Alan. I just couldn't take your rejection anymore. I needed to see you. But you wouldn't let me. I needed for you to tell me everything would be okay, just like you did before."

Molly relaxed, but only slightly, as she stood in her bra, with her pants undone, her top shredded on the floor at her feet. Her breathing had slowed, but she was still aware of its ragged sound. Perhaps because she had come too close to not breathing ever again.

"I think she came here to kill you," she told Alan.

He squinted at her.

"She was already in the apartment when I came by. The door was ajar. Then, when I came inside, she accosted me."

"She's lying!" Astrid charged. "That whore is incapable of uttering one truthful word."

"Then what were you doing inside my apartment, Astrid?"

Molly saw that he left off *with a knife* from his question.

Astrid stared at the item in her hand as if seeing it for the first time.

"The question is, I think, what is *she* doing here?" Astrid pointed the knife in Molly's direction.

Molly took a step back even though the bed still separated her from the woman.

"Isn't it bad enough my husband screwed her? Did you have to screw her, too?"

"Astrid," Alan said slowly, "that's not Claire Laraway. That's her sister, Molly."

She looked from him to Molly, then back again.

Then she began shaking her head. “Oh, Alan. You were the only who never lied to me. Why did you have to start now?”

Then with a shrill, guttural scream, she charged him, knife held above her head. Alan caught the arm holding the dangerous weapon, but Astrid kicked and hit at him in a way that made Molly wince. Then she grabbed the knife with her free hand and swiped at him, penetrating the arm of his coat. He stumbled backward, grasping the area.

“Alan!” Molly rushed forward.

Astrid switched the knife to her right hand and waved it wildly at Molly. “You’re next, whore.”

She advanced on her. Molly lifted her linen-covered right arm, fending off a glance from the sharp blade.

Then Alan caught Astrid from behind, and Molly reached up and twisted the knife from her hand. It landed with a dull clatter on the floor.

Alan met Molly’s gaze. She couldn’t be sure what she saw there. Sadness, maybe. Relief.

“Astrid Hodge, you’re under arrest for the murder of Claire Laraway and Valerie Chevalier. You have the right to remain silent….”

# 23

I STOOD ON THE OTHER side of the two-sided mirror, staring at the scene in the interrogation room. Prosecutor Bill Grissom stood next to me, jingling spare change with his hand in the pocket of his expensive slacks. Normally, as the detective in charge, I would have been the one questioning Captain Seymour Hodge. But if ever there was a conflict of interest, it definitely applied here. So instead I watched as John Roche interrogated him.

Although it wasn't so much an interrogation as a monologue. On Hodge's part.

"If you're going to arrest anyone, let it be me," he said, looking somehow smaller in the room, his presence diminished by his words, by his guilt. "It's all my fault. I had that affair and Astrid just…snapped. Something happened and she changed."

Grissom leaned closer to me. "So what do you think she did? Is it possible she harvested his sperm and inserted it into his dead mistress's and your ex-wife's bodies in order to set him up for the crimes? You think the hairs we found in the wounds match his?"

I rubbed my closed eyelids. I could have done without the imagery. “I don’t know. But I think after Claire Laraway showed up dead, he had to have suspected something.”

“Aiding and abetting?”

I looked at the prosecutor. He seemed out to get blood on this one. As far as I was concerned, too much blood had been spilled already.

I thought of Molly and how close she had come to being number three on Astrid’s list.

“I think the guy’s already paying enough, don’t you?”

In fact, Hodge seemed riddled with guilt. And surely his career was over. Couldn’t have the wife of a captain going around killing people. Didn’t reflect well on the department.

“I knew it was a woman.”

I stared at Grissom.

“The security video of the black-cloaked figure coming out of the Josephine. Helps that she was wearing the same clothes tonight. Should wrap up everything nice and neat.”

“Yeah. Congratulations,” I said, heading for the door.

“Where you going? You’re the one who cracked this case. Don’t you want to stick around and enjoy the spoils?”

“I think I’ll pass.”

Truth was, I wasn’t feeling very triumphant. Yes,

while a killer was no longer roaming the streets, I had been indirectly responsible for Val's death. For whatever godforsaken reason, Astrid had gotten it into her head that the reason I didn't want to see her had to do with my ex. Maybe she'd been following me. Maybe she'd seen us having lunch together. Maybe she'd known someone had stayed the night at my apartment and had assumed it was Val.

Whatever the reason, had I never slept with Astrid Hodge, my ex would still be alive.

Unfortunately Claire Laraway wouldn't have been so lucky.

I shook my head, wondering at the way some women's minds worked. So her husband had had an affair with a younger woman. It wasn't like that had never been heard of before. And since Claire had spent the night with Claude Lafitte, it had been a pretty good indicator that her relationship with Hodge was over.

Then again, you had to consider the woman. Astrid Hodge had been top-shelf at one time. Crème de la crème. The woman every man watched when she entered a room. But, of course, that was all temporary when you looked at the whole picture. Time saw to that. Once you got into your forties, there was always someone younger, someone prettier than you. I guess for a woman like Astrid, who had built her entire world and relationship around her looks, having that fact rubbed in her face had made her snap.

And I hadn't helped.

I walked out of the precinct and stood in the bright midmorning sunlight. No, I didn't feel like celebrating. I felt like having a good, strong drink.

Even more, I felt like seeing Molly.

"SO THAT'S IT, THEN," Molly said as she sat across from me at Tujague's.

I found it interesting that I'd taken her to the place that had essentially started our affair.

I'd gotten the name of the new hotel she was staying at and called her, asking her to meet me at the restaurant. I figured we could kill two birds with one stone. Over a great meal I could tell her everything that had happened, down to Hodge's interrogation. And by then I'd hopefully have a handle on my unsettled feelings about the whole shebang.

Damn, she looked good. She'd taken a shower and had changed into a pair of neat slacks that fit her just so and a blouse that was frilly and sexy, the white complementing her pale skin and hair, which she wore loose.

I avoided looking at her neck and the few light bruises there, caused by Astrid's choking her—which reminded me that it could have been much worse.

I nodded. "Yes, that's it."

I'd explained to her—hesitant beginning to bitter end—what had happened and how. She'd nodded here and there but had kept quiet, seeming to be far away from the table filled with food. Hell, my own mind wasn't on the food, either. And my mind was always on food at Tujague's.

She reached out and touched my hand. Her skin was warm and soft against mine. "Thank you."

"For what?"

She glanced down at the tablecloth. "For including me. For taking the time to tell me everything when it couldn't have been easy for you."

I shifted, and the movement caused her to remove her hand. I missed it as soon as it was gone.

She said, "None of this is your fault. You know that, don't you?"

I stared out the window at the people passing on the street, then at the customers inside the restaurant. "You can't ignore the role I played, Molly. Had I not slept with Astrid…had I just talked to her when she wanted to talk…maybe…"

"Maybe Valerie would still be alive?"

I winced, realizing the futile nature of my thoughts.

I'd never been one to play the game "what if." Facts were facts. I looked at Molly's beautiful face across from mine. And the fact here: Molly was ten times more woman than I deserved.

"So…" she began slowly. "Where do we go from here?"

I squinted at her. I hadn't expected her to come out and ask me a question of that nature. Women tended to be savvier about stuff like that nowadays.

And men didn't come more commitment-phobic than me.

Hey, all you had to do was look over the past year to know that whatever I touched turned to chaos when it came to women.

"We both go back to life as it was before, I guess."

Even as I said the words, I felt a stabbing pain in my chest. Almost like an ice pick. It reminded me of the wound on my arm. I looked at where the overcoat I was wearing had been cut, the bandage visible underneath.

"I see," she said so quietly I almost didn't hear her.

She began to stand up.

I suppressed the desire to get up with her. Desire? Hell, it took every ounce of energy I had.

"I guess this is goodbye then."

I nodded and traced a line on the tablecloth with my thumb. "Goodbye."

She stood for long moments, as if waiting for me to say something else. Then she gathered her purse and turned to walk away.

"Oh, Molly?" I said.

She stopped but didn't turn back to me.

"I just wanted to say, you know, thanks for what you did with Zoe."

Nothing, until she uttered a simple, "You're welcome."

Then the best damn thing that ever happened to me walked right out of my life. And, stupid fool that I am, I let her.

MOLLY SAT ON THE PLANE, staring through the window unseeingly. She'd managed to get on the next flight out, which was later that night. It hadn't been difficult. Her things had still been packed from her move from one hotel to another. And she'd had plenty of time to see to a couple of additional items.

She'd thought about calling her mother, letting her know she was coming home. Then she'd wondered what the use would be. She'd probably ask what kind of souvenirs she'd picked up for her. Her mother wouldn't understand that this hadn't been a vacation. This trip had been about bringing Claire's killer to justice. And she'd seen to that.

But she was taking home one souvenir, wasn't she? A broken heart.

She leaned her forehead against the glass and closed her eyes as the engines geared up for takeoff.

Home. She was going home.

She waited for relief to hit her. For the guilt about how distant her relationship with her sister had become to abate. Instead she felt a weight heavier than the aircraft itself parked on her shoulders.

Images from her visit to the Big Easy glided through her mind like a slide show. Waiting for Alan outside his apartment and sticking her purse in his door to prevent him from closing it…going to the Goth bar and watching Alan become jealous at the attention she was getting from other men…their naked bodies joining in a kind of union she hadn't known until now could exist.

Well, she thought, sitting back and sighing. That was going to help, wasn't it?

She plucked at the flight magazine in the pocket in front of her and flipped the pages. Only she couldn't see anything past the hot tears that had flooded her eyes.

Goodbye, Claire. Goodbye, New Orleans.

Goodbye, Alan.

THIS HAD TO BE ONE OF the longest days of my life. Of course, it probably didn't help that I hadn't gotten any sleep last night. Still, even though it was ten o'clock, I didn't think I'd be getting any sleep tonight, either.

I'd covered a lot in one day. I'd sorted through everything in the Quarter Killer case, sat down to dinner with Zoe and the latest addition to the family, aka her husband, then helped Emilie and Laure see to Val's funeral arrangements—a black event scheduled two days from now that I wasn't looking forward to. But every time I blinked, Molly came to mind.

By now she'd be on a plane back home. If she wasn't home already. I'd called the hotel before going to the girls' place and asked to be put through to her room. Not to talk to her. Rather, I'd just wanted to see if she was there.

The hotel operator had explained that she'd already checked out.

I trudged up the stairs to my apartment, the slit in my coat sleeve catching my attention. While I'd changed the shirt underneath before going to dinner, I didn't know what I was going to do about the constant reminder of what had transpired last night.

Or what I was going to do about the constant reminders of Molly everywhere I looked.

Oh, I had no physical reminders. Our affair had been too brief for that. But I'd read somewhere that to love an hour was to love a lifetime. I'd thought the comment idiotic at the time. Now I knew how true it was.

I got my keys out as I neared the door. A sound came from inside my apartment.

The first thing I thought of was last night, when I'd come back to find Astrid holding a knife on Molly. Now, putting down the leftovers Zoe had packed for me, I slid my firearm from its holster and unlocked the door as quietly as possible…then stood looking at the last thing I would have expected to find.

A dog.

I looked back out into the hall, then inside again, certain I was seeing things. The black and white pup gave a bark, then ran behind the couch, peering out at me. I slowly put away my gun, picked up the leftovers, then closed the door.

Christ. What was the world coming to when someone broke into your house and left a puppy behind?

I spotted an item hanging on the back of the

bathroom door. An overcoat exactly like the one I had on. But new, the tags still hanging from the sleeve, a note pinned to the collar. I neared it, noticing the way the dog scrambled backward, his nails clicking on the wood floor as he went, his tongue lolling out of his mouth. He barked again, the force of which caused him to ricochet back a full foot.

I shook my head and cursed as I tore the note from the coat and opened it.

*Alan. The coat is a gift from me to you. Wear it in good health. Rourke, well…Rourke needed a home. And you needed something to help turn your house into a home. Take care of him and yourself for me. Love, Molly.*

I walked into the kitchen, where Molly had spread papers out on the floor. There was business next to it but not on it. I scratched my chin. Then again, I supposed it was better than in the middle of my sofa.

Also put out were two dog bowls, one with dry food, the other with water. I put the leftovers on the counter, then rummaged through them. I found a slice of meat loaf and tore off a piece.

"Here doggy, doggy," I said, crouching down and holding out the meat.

A small furry head popped around the corner, though the rest of his body remained hidden.

"Come here, you mangy mutt," I said under my

breath, then smiled and waved the meat. "Are you hungry?"

The rest of his plump body appeared, and he leaned forward and appeared to lie down. I didn't realize he was scooting closer to me until the distance began to disappear.

Finally he was near enough to take the meat. But he didn't.

"Here," I said, placing it closer to his mouth.

He tentatively sniffed it but didn't take it.

I looked at the meat. "Yeah," I said. "That's about my take on it, too."

I sighed, then scooped up the fur ball, holding him up to stare into his big, watery brown eyes as he stared back.

Then he licked my chin and wagged his little tail simultaneously, nearly wiggling straight out of my hand.

I chuckled and held him out farther. I held a finger up. "Now, if you're going to be staying here, we're going to have to lay down some ground rules. Number one is no licking of the face. I don't know where your tongue has been."

So he licked my finger.

I put him back down and shrugged out of my coat, watching as the pup went around and around my ankles.

Rourke. Only Molly would do something so thoughtful after I'd essentially treated her like crap.

And all I could think of were ways to make it up

to her. Because one thing I was sure of, as the little terror barked and pulled at the hem of my pants, was that I wasn't going to be stuck taking care of the pup alone.

# 24

MOLLY HAD BEEN HOME a week. And if she hadn't exactly forgotten about New Orleans, she was at least going through the motions of getting back to her old routine.

She sighed as she parked her car in front of the one-hundred-and-twenty-year-old house in the Old West neighborhood that she'd chosen over a swanky new condo on the outskirts of town. All around her the leaves were changing color, filling the air with the pungent smell of autumn. She got out, collected her purse and a bag of groceries, then locked up before heading for the three-story structure that had once been a single house but had been renovated and divided into condos five years ago. Her place kept the atmosphere of the old nineteenth-century house, with fireplaces in the living room and bedroom, large and airy rooms and natural woodwork throughout.

Since returning to Toledo, this had been the most difficult part of the day. At work she could find ways to keep busy, keep her mind occupied so she didn't think of Alan so much. But when she got home… well, it seemed Alan was the only thing she could think about.

She'd really never noticed how empty her life had been before. How lonely. She'd been content to work at the job of her choice, volunteer at the Red Cross two hours a week, come home to make a simple dinner, then either read a book or catch the latest episode of one of her favorite TV shows.

Now…

Well, now she saw herself in a way that only stepping outside her normal existence could have made possible. And she didn't much like what she saw. She knew she needed to make some changes, but for the life of her, she couldn't think of what. She supposed she could take a couple of classes that had nothing to do with her job. Try a hobby. Maybe take up running. Forge a closer relationship with her mother and her new family.

Still, none of that seemed capable of filling the void that had taken up residence around her heart.

She unlocked the outer door, then checked her mailbox among the line of others. Nothing but junk mail. She tucked it into the grocery bag, then moved up the stairs, noticing the slightly musty smell that came with the old place. She let herself inside her apartment.

"Hello, Molly."

She turned so fast she dropped the bag of groceries.

There, sitting on her couch, wearing his new trench coat and worrying his hat in his hands, sat Alan.

She moved her free hand over her heart. "God. You scared the daylights out of me."

He smiled slightly, then got up.

He looked good. More than good. He looked great. His hair was neat and combed. His handsome face freshly shaved. And nowhere on his person was a single wrinkle.

Molly waited for her heart rate to settle down, then realized it probably wouldn't. Because while what had triggered it initially may have been fear, coming home to find Alan in her apartment made her heart pound with hope.

She busied herself with collecting the groceries that had scattered over the floor. "What are you doing here?"

"And here I thought your first question would be how did I get in," he said, closer than she expected. She stood up to find him right in front of her. He chuckled softly. "Then again, you never did ask the type of questions I expected you to. Which is probably why I'm having such a damn hard time getting you out of my mind."

Molly didn't know what to say. Alan was standing right here in her apartment, fulfilling every wish she would never have dared say aloud, and all she could think about was how out of place he looked.

"How *did* you get in?" she asked.

"We cops have a few tricks up our sleeves." He shrugged.

"What'd you do with Rourke?"

"Zoe's looking after him at the house."

She nodded, happy on a level she couldn't explore just then that he'd kept the puppy she'd adopted for him from Akela and Claude. She couldn't bear the thought of leaving Alan the way he'd been. Which was as lonely as she was.

"How did *you* get in?" it was his turn to ask.

"I sweet-talked your landlord," she said with the smile that had likely won him over.

He shifted his feet. "Look, Molly, I'm not going to pretend that I think my being here is right…."

She searched his eyes, wondering where he was going.

"Truth is, I think I'm the last person you should be involved with."

"Why?" she asked.

He blinked as if the answer should be obvious. "I'm older than you, for one."

She crossed her arms. "So?"

"I have a lot of emotional baggage."

"Don't we all?"

He looked down at the hat he still held and smiled. "You're not going to make this easy for me, are you?"

"If you came here to ease your conscience by dumping me all over again, Alan, then no."

He lifted his gaze to hers. "But that's not why I'm here."

Her heart skipped a beat.

"You see, despite everything I just said and every damn argument I make to myself, the truth is I don't want to go another day without you in my life."

Before Molly knew that was she was going to do, she was nestled in the warm cradle of his arms, her cheek pressed against his shoulder.

"Jesus, how I've missed you," he murmured, and she felt his lips on her hair. "I've missed this."

She had, too. So much that she suspected she was about to cry.

There had been so little warmth in her life. And she understood now that she was partially to blame for that. Every time her sister had tried to get closer to her, she'd pushed her away. Perhaps as a type of self-defense mechanism to prevent herself from getting hurt. Or maybe because she hadn't known any differently.

But as she held Alan, she knew an incredible desire to change that. She wanted to start reaching out. Touching people. Letting them touch her. Because to do otherwise would be a disservice to the lesson she'd learned. A lesson Claire had taught her. That life was precious. And that she needed to live every sweet moment of it to the fullest.

"Molly, I can't promise that I'll always be the man you want me to be."

She pulled back. "I never asked you to be anyone other than who you are, Alan."

He brushed the backs of his knuckles over her cheek. "I know that. But when I'm a heel to you… well, I feel like the worst jerk on earth."

"So don't be a heel."

He grinned at her. "You make it sound like all this is simple."

"It is, isn't it?"

He looked dubious.

"You're here, Alan. That means you want me, not just for a night or two. And since we've already established that I want you…well, where's the problem?"

His gaze skimmed over her face, lingering on her mouth. "Oh, the fact that you live in Toledo is one."

"Not if I move down to New Orleans to be with you."

He squinted at her.

"Alan, I want you to be in my life. And if moving is what it takes, just tell me when the next flight is."

He stared at her, then kissed her suddenly, as if he couldn't quite believe what she was saying but was awfully glad of it.

He took her hand and led her toward the door.

She laughed. "Where are we going?"

"To the airport. I don't want to leave Rourke alone with Zoe for too long. She'll corrupt him. He'll forget all the rules I've been teaching him."

Molly dug in her heels, then pulled him back to

her, kissing him hungrily, erasing the past week, making up for lost time.

"He'll be okay," she whispered, nipping his bottom lip.

Then she took his hand and led him toward the king-size bed in her bedroom.

I WATCHED HER SHAPELY backside as she led the way, wearing a grin I didn't think I'd be able to wash away with lime soap.

What a woman, huh? And while I still didn't know what god I'd pleased to deserve this incredible gift, I vowed to spend the rest of my life thanking him for it.